ALIEN SWARM

The concussion from the grenades sent alien limbs, heads, and bodies everywhere, and shook the roof of the hangar.

But the bugs just kept coming.

Climbing over hundreds of their own dead, they poured into the room.

"Fall back," Green shouted to his men and they started moving, firing as they went.

"Give them cover!" Joyce shouted, and she and her crew did the best they could to keep the bugs back.

But it was clear Green and his men weren't going to make it. Green had been right. There were just too many of them.

The situation was hopeless.

But Joyce kept firing anyway.

ALIENS™

ROGUE

Sandy Schofield

Adapted from the Dark Horse comic Rogue
Written by Ian Edington
Art by Will Simpson

MILLENNIUM

Orion Paperbacks
A Millennium Book
First published in Great Britain in 1996 by Orion Books Ltd,
Orion House, 5 Upper St Martin's Lane, London WC2H 9EA

A CIP catalogue record for this book is available
from the British Library.

ISBN: 1 85798 412 9

Printed and bound in Great Britain by
Clays Ltd, St Ives plc

For Steve Perry
one of the finest writers of them all.

ALIENS

ROGUE

1

The dreams faded like mist on an early fall morning. Real dreams, the kind you can feel, taste, and know you're there. She tried to hold the image of her two children, smiling, laughing. A park, green grass, swings, and happiness. Drake and Cass happy, swinging, up and down, up and down. She wanted to pull the feelings close, hold them against her chest like she would her children. Warm sunshine, the smell of freshly mowed grass, the sound of laughter, all mixed in the comforting feeling of home and family.

Real dreams. Real memories.

But dreams and memories nonetheless.

The harder she tried to grasp the dream, the

1

thinner, the more distant it became. She reached out for ten-year-old Drake, but his face lit up in playful laughter as he kept swinging and she couldn't seem to catch him. She watched him swing until finally all the pleasant feelings were gone.

The trees, the green grass, the park, were gone. Drake, his smile, his happiness, were gone.

Cass was gone, replaced by the cold of the sleep chamber and the oily, metallic smell of the transport ship.

Captain Joyce Palmer groaned and fingered the open button for her chamber. The hiss of escaping gas clouded the air for a moment with a blue frozen mist. She forced herself to sit up and swing her legs over the edge. Around her the machines of the transport vessel *Caliban* did their silent work. Slowly she looked around, afraid of what she might see after seven months. The control panels above each of the cold-sleep chambers all showed green and the auxiliary flight board at the front of the room was the same. Everything seemed normal and running, and she let the dread ease away much like the dream had done.

She looked down at her bare legs and for just a moment she felt dizzy. She gripped the edge of the chamber with both hands and it passed quickly, just as it did every time she came out of the damn ice boxes. She hated cold sleep.

She pulled in as large a breath as her lungs would allow and then shivered. The cold had invaded every part of her body and she hated it. She fought to bring back just a little of the feeling of the warm sunshine and the smell of the grass in the park. But the dream stayed just outside her grasp and finally she gave up, taking another deep breath and letting the shaking cold overwhelm her for a moment.

Finally, as the shivering passed, she glanced up again at an auxiliary flight board that showed the status of the ship and its location. She studied it for a moment. All lights green. It appeared they were dropping out of Einsteinian Space right on schedule. No problems, at least that she could see.

She took one more deep breath as beside her Deegan, her copilot, raised the lid on his sleep chamber. Beyond Deegan was the chamber in which their only passenger, Mr. Cray, still slept. The lights on his chamber were also still green and showing progress in the wake-up cycle.

"You all right, boss?" Deegan said without sitting up, his voice hoarse and thick, like he sounded after a hard night of drinking.

She just nodded and rubbed her face.

Unlike her own thin and trim body, Deegan was more of a jellyfish out of water. While she watched her weight and worked out daily, he ate too much, drank too much, and never exercised. He had white, pasty skin and the cold sleep every trip really got to him. She told him that if he kept himself in better shape, it wouldn't be so bad, but he never listened.

She slowly stood, the metal deck ice-cold under her bare feet. She quickly slipped on her sandals and then stretched, loosening sore muscles in her shoulders and back. She wore only brief bikini underwear and a light tank top. Goose bumps formed on her brown skin as she fought to loosen the muscles and shake the chill from the cold sleep. Even though she was in the best condition she could maintain, it would still take her hours, even after a long hot shower and a half hour of exercise to fully get beyond the chill. That was her pattern after cold sleep. It never seemed to vary so she might as well get it started.

She glanced again at the flight board. They were six hours out from Charon Base. Just the thought of that name gave her chills. She hated it there almost more than she hated cold sleep. She sighed. "Last trip," she promised herself under her breath. She had more than enough time to take an extra hot shower after exercising. She had the feeling she was going to need it.

She gathered up her brown cloth slacks, brown vest, and the Harley-Davidson baseball cap that held her long black hair out of her face. Then she moved over and looked down through the cover of the sleep chamber at Mr. Cray. He was on his back, clad only in his boxer shorts. He looked to be in good shape, with strong chest and arm muscles and a trim waist. His head lolled slightly to one side and his mouth was partially open. Her guess was that in normal sleep he snored. She caught herself hoping she would get the chance to find out.

"Deegan," she said, patting the lid of Cray's chamber. "Make sure our guest gets up. We don't want him asleep for the big meeting with Professor Kleist." With a final glance at his solid chest and the bulge in his boxer shorts, she headed toward her cabin and her wonderfully warm shower.

Behind her she heard Deegan moan, "Yes,

boss." Then there was an even louder moan as he sat up.

On Charon Base, in a small wood and metal-lined corridor carved out of solid rock years earlier by prisoners, five Marines in full battle armor gathered. Helmets locked on, faceplates up, automatic Kramer rifles slung over shoulders. Taser Web rifles in their hands, they looked like they were ready to go into a war.

And that's exactly what they were preparing to do.

The corridor dead-ended into a metal, airlock-style door. The white plates of the battle armor contrasted sharply with the brown carpet on the floor and the gray steel of the airlock. The corridor had a slight smell of sweat and fear as it did before any mission.

Sergeant Green, not the tallest of the five Marines, but by far the largest and most powerful in shoulder width and the huge size of his arms, waited until all were silent before he gave them their mission. "We're after an adult warrior, alive and intact. I know that stinks, but that's the drill."

He made a point of looking around at the three men and Boone, the only woman left on his squad. No one answered and he smiled to himself. They didn't like this shit any more than he did, but they would follow their orders and that was what he needed at the moment. He was following his orders, and they needed to follow theirs if they planned on getting out of this alive.

He went on. "Taser Webs only. Kramers slung unless on my order. Is that understood?"

Private McPhillips said, "Yes, sir," softly, and no one else moved.

"Dillon, the Sound Cannon ready?"

"Warming up, sir. Just hope the thing works this time."

"Don't we all," Sergeant Green said. This was another stupid mission, but when the Professor said do something, they did it. That was their assignment no matter how bad or wrong it was. Or how many lives it cost them.

"Let's do it. McPhillips, take the point. The rest of you keep it tight."

McPhillips turned and punched the open cycle on the airlock doors that divided the human areas of Charon Base from the alien hive. Thick, hot air blasted the Marines as McPhillips quickly checked both sides of the passage ahead and then slowly moved forward, checking above the door and the ceiling down the rock corridor.

Charon Base was not much more than a large hunk of solid rock orbiting a class-three yellow star in an elliptical orbit. Originally it had been a government prison camp, used to hold the most dangerous criminals from Earth. The prisoners' jobs were to dig more tunnels, expand the base continuously with useless tunnel after useless tunnel. The rock was honeycombed with tunnels fifteen, sometimes twenty levels deep. Most of the prisoners had died doing their "make-work" job.

After the alien invasion of Earth and its recapture, the government didn't have the money or the desire to ship prisoners out this far, so Z.C.T. Corporation bought Charon Base and started the top-secret Project Chimera.

A section of the old tunnels were then sealed

off from the rest of the base and five captured aliens and one queen were let loose to form the beginnings of a hive.

Another small section near the surface was upgraded to the highest human living standards and top scientists from around the inhabited planets were hired and brought in, along with a platoon of government Marines to help deal with the bugs and safeguard the government interest.

The rest of the tunnels were left, forgotten for the most part.

Professor John Kleist was put in charge of finding as many ways as possible to make a profit from the aliens. From the acid blood to the royal jelly. Everything. But Professor Kleist had taken the project beyond even the corporation's fondest dreams. And that progress had come at a high price, paid mostly by the lives of the Marines.

Sergeant Green kicked in his suit's air filters as the thick, rotting alien smell filled the air. Someone once described an alien hive's odor as ten thousand rotten eggs frying in rancid grease. Green had done a hundred missions into hives in the war since he had heard that description. Without fail every time that smell hit him he thought of that image. And then thought it wasn't a strong enough description. Not by far. Thank God for body armor and the filters.

The five white-armor-covered Marines moved forward slowly as the corridor widened beyond the human section and became a large rock tunnel after about twenty meters. It felt to Green like an old train tunnel, only with higher ceilings.

McPhillips, at point, stepped gingerly around puddles of alien slime, picking a path one careful step at a time. The acid slime coated the walls and dripped from the ceiling forming odd pockets of blackness. The Marines' lanterns couldn't penetrate those pockets. It was those pockets that were so dangerous. Aliens slept in those holes and could appear and strike without notice at lightning speed.

"Stay alert," Green said, his voice suddenly sounding hollow in his headset, even to his own ears.

McPhillips, with the shorter Dillon right behind him, continued to pick a careful path through the mess. The new battle armor was good, but it wasn't perfect. Enough of the acid and it could be eaten right through to the skin.

Green glanced back at Choi and Boone as the airlock slid closed behind them. There was a reason Boone was the last surviving woman in his platoon. She was as tough as nails and damn near as fast as a bug on reaction time. She and the red-headed, skinny Choi were inseparable, both being from New York, both being about the same age. The men kidded them about making love like rabbits, but it never seemed to get to them. They just went right ahead and did it, at all times of the day or night.

"Watch the walls," he said to Boone, nodding his head to the right at some extra deep pockets of alien slime. "Choi, keep an eye on those side corridors. We don't want one of the bastards getting in behind us."

"You got it, sir," Choi said.

Green took a deep breath and let it out slowly. His stomach was twisting up, but so far everything was standard.

Another thirty slow, careful meters into the hive. Nothing but them moving. "I don't want to go much farther into this," Green said. Behind him the gray doors of the airlock seemed an impossible distance away. In front of him McPhillips stopped but didn't turn around. "Dillon, any traces on the scanner?"

"Blank as Choi's brain," Dillon said. "Nothing at all—"

The scream filled Green's headset. Oh, God. No! He had heard screams like that far too often over the years.

Instinctively he dropped and spun, his rifle off his shoulder, up and aimed.

"Boone! Cut it loose!" Choi's cry echoed with Boone's scream as the huge alien warrior dragged her up the wall toward its hole in the ceiling.

Like the well-trained Marine that she was, Boone knew some tricks of her own. Kicking out with her boots at the alien's head and arms, she twisted in the alien's sharp claws.

Right, then left, always moving.

Twisting, trying to get an arm free from the alien's grasp to get a shot at the bug's arm or head, anything to get it to drop her.

As if in the worst slow motion of a nightmare gone bad, Green watched in sick fascination, not daring to fire until he had a clear shot at the head or knees of the bug.

Choi looked like he almost might have an open shot at the bug's legs in a second.

Boone twisted to aim her Taser Web at the bug's head.

She almost made it.

But before she or Choi or anyone could get a

shot off, the worst happened. Huge, saliva-filled outer jaws snapped open and the second alien jaws from deep in its throat shot through Boone's armored helmet like it was so much tissue.

Her final scream echoed and then died like someone had cut off the power on a stereo.

Pieces of her helmet, face, and brains exploded over the corridor, raining down on everyone, covering Choi in his lover's blood. Her body twitched in the alien's grasp, still fighting, even though her head was gone.

The alien's smaller jaws retreated into its throat, pulling along the dome of Boone's brains and face.

"No!" Choi screamed. Like all of them he had his rifle unholstered, working for a shot at the alien that wouldn't leave Boone covered in acid blood.

But now that didn't matter and before Green could even react, Choi fired. His shot hit the bug head-on in the body with a full charge.

The bug exploded like a kid's firecracker, raining acid down the walls and onto the corridor. Boone's body dropped to the stone floor, one hand and arm of the alien still attached around her waist. She bounced once among the remains of the bug's body and came to rest on her side, her back to the corridor, her hair filling the hole in the back of her helmet.

Green reached Choi a second too late to stop him. "Hold your fire, God damn it!" He slapped Choi's gun aside.

"Boone . . ." Choi said, and started toward her acid-soaked remains.

Green held his arm. "She's gone and now you

might have killed us all." Green held on as Choi
fought to pull away and go to Boone.

"Sarge!" Dillon shouted. "I got signals! Readings
coming in all over. From three sides—"

There was a high-pitched, panicked sound to
Dillon's voice and McPhillips said, "Shit!" loud
enough to echo in Green's head gear.

"Damn it!" Green shook Choi hard, snapping
him around and away from the sight of Boone's
body. "We just gave them all a wake-up call, and
now they're coming down for breakfast. Get your
ass ready to fight."

He glanced quickly around at McPhillips and
Dillon, then shouted, "Combat spacing front and
rear. Hustle! Dillon, the Sound Cannon?"

"Prepared and ready, sir. Max. frequency, wide
field focus."

"Let's hope the damn thing works this time,"
Green said under his breath. Louder he said,
"Taser Webs, stand by."

It seemed like only a second before the corridor, the walls around them, the tunnels to the
sides of them, came alive with wave after wave of
ugly, mad bugs. Every one of them five to six
times their size. Green could hear the rustling of
their movements even through his armor's shell.
He'd always heard the old saying that if the aliens'
rustlings and clickings were loud enough to penetrate armor, you were as good as dead because
there were so many of them.

This time seemed like it wasn't going to be an
exception to the rule. Green couldn't remember
seeing so many bugs in one fight. Straight on,
without the Sound Cannon, the four of them
would never stand a chance.

"Dillon, fire!"

The long metal Sound Cannon looked more like an old bazooka from the Earth wars than anything else. It seemed to jump slightly in Dillon's hand, but there was no sound. No explosion from its end. And for what seemed like an eternity, nothing happened.

Green watched as Dillon focused on the dial on the top of the weapon, nodding, ignoring the certain death around him.

The gun seemed to be aimed at nothing in particular. Around them the air in the tight rock chamber seemed to be shimmering, as if waves of heat were coming off hot pavement. The alien saliva formations wavered in Green's eyes, but he knew it was nothing more than the surface effects of the Sound Cannon. It was working. He almost wanted to scream with joy.

Every bug in the corridor froze, saliva dripping from wide mouths.

"God, I love that thing," Green said, letting out the breath he was holding. "Damned if I know how it works, but when it does, it gets them every time."

Somehow Professor Kleist had discovered a weapon that got to the creatures' nervous systems and froze them like so many ugly statues in an alien park. The problem was that it couldn't always be counted on and very seldom worked for longer than sixty seconds. The Professor kept promising he was working on making it better, more reliable, but in the meantime Green had lost more than half his platoon. But this time it looked like the Sound Cannon, as they all called it, had saved their lives.

At least all but Boone's.

He pointed to the biggest and closest warrior on the corridor wall. "Web that one and let's get out of here."

Dillon's and McPhillips's two Taser Webs fired at the same moment, pulling the huge, stunned warrior off the wall with a loud, smacking thump. Surrounded in nets that not even the acid blood of the aliens or their super strength could eat through, it lay on the corridor floor, drooling.

Beep! Beep! Beep!

"Shit!" Dillon said as the sound echoed through the rock chamber like the timer of a bomb.

Green knew that sound. It was the sound of their funeral if they didn't move damn fast.

"Sarge," Dillon managed to choke out, his voice trembling more than Green had ever heard it before. "This damn thing is malfunctioning. We've got about thirty seconds before it blows and sends us and this entire station into space."

"Choi," Green shouted at where the Marine stood over his lover's body. "Help with that bug. Now!"

Beep! Beep! Beep! Beep!

The sound echoed off the stone walls and the frozen aliens around them, increasing in tempo and matching Green's racing heart. He knew it was the sound of the clock ticking away their final seconds of life.

Faster and faster with each beep.

With a final look at Boone, Choi did as he was ordered. He turned and was beside McPhillips almost instantly, yanking on the webs around the bug.

Dillon backed slowly toward the airlock holding the Sound Cannon.

Green kept both his Taser Web in his right hand and his Kramer automatic rifle in his left covering the frozen aliens as Choi and McPhillips dragged the stunned warrior down the corridor as fast as they could go.

Beep! Beep! Beep! Beep! Beep!

"Fifteen seconds," Dillon said. "I got to shut it down or it'll blow."

"Hold on as long as you can," Green said. "Then run!"

Beep! Beep! Beep! Beep! Beep!

"You're telling me," Dillon shouted back. Quickly he was backing toward the entrance and Green was matching him step for step.

Beep! Beep! Beep! Beep! Beep! Beep!

"Shit! Not much longer—"

"Hold it!" Green shouted.

"Eight, seven, six—"

"Hold it!"

The beeps had almost become one long scream echoing off the slime formations and the stone walls. Another few seconds and the explosion would destroy the entire base.

"I'm shutting it down!"

Green, still backing up beside Dillon, glanced around.

Choi and McPhillips had the warrior to the airlock. Another few seconds and they would be through and to safety.

He and Dillon had backed to within twenty meters of the lock, but that might be twenty meters too far if the bugs around and in front of them reacted very fast.

Dillon clicked off the cannon, stuffed the long tube under his arm, turned, and ran.

The silence in the corridor seemed almost as loud as the beeping.

Green waited for just a moment as the bugs started to move, slowly at first, then angry as hell, before he also turned and ran behind Dillon, keeping right with him every step.

Choi and McPhillips had the captured warrior through the airlock and had come back to the lock with Taser Webs aimed over the two running Marines.

Green sucked in lungful after lungful of air and did his best to run as fast as he could, his body armor pounding every joint in his body. These suits just weren't meant for exercise.

Ahead, Choi and McPhillips pointed Tasers at him. He trusted them to be good shots, but he still didn't much like how they were aiming straight at him.

Dillon cleared the airlock as McPhillips fired, barely missing Green and connecting with a bug that was too damn close behind him.

Green figured at that moment he was dead. His heart was pounding so hard that he felt like it might explode—that is if a bug didn't grab him first.

Choi punched the airlock close command and the doors started to grind together.

Green dove headfirst through the closing airlock, tumbling like a white ball of armor as Choi fired another Taser at the closest bug. Green stopped his tumble and lay on the carpeted floor, face-to-face with the captured warrior, trying to catch his breath.

Saliva dripped off the bug's open jaws and Green caught a glimpse of its interior jaw in that black hole of a throat. It was aimed right at his head.

He quickly scrambled to his feet and moved a few meters away, where he did his best to suck as much air as he could get into his lungs.

Too close.

Just too goddamned close.

2

Professor Kleist leaned back in his chair, his fingers steepled in front of him, his bright blue eyes focused intently on the wall of monitors in front of his glass desk. Fifty-meter-square screens filled the huge wall, all following one activity or another around the base. If the Professor wanted, he could divide each screen by four or eight or even sixteen, all showing different scenes. It was the most sophisticated security system available in the corporation and since the system's installment he had upgraded it considerably. It was one of his most prized tools and he spent many hours in front of it, just watching the fifteen hundred people under his command.

With system, no one on Charon Base

sneezed, whispered, or made love without him knowing about it.

As with many things on Charon Base, the Professor had seen to every detail of the construction of his office. On Earth the almost gymnasium-size room would have been considered excessive. The oak walls and shelves a frivolity, the thick carpet almost too plush.

In one corner was a full kitchen, always stocked with fresh food and drink. Shelves of real books—research, reference, and fiction—filled two walls. Those books were his personal collection and it had taken most of one transport ship's capacity just to get them here. But it had been a small expense in exchange for his needs and what he had accomplished for the corporation so far.

But the central feature of the office was the huge oak desk and high-backed chair facing the wall of monitors—a wall that curved slightly such that there was nothing else in view, like a surround vision movie, only those screens weren't showing a film.

The surface of the desk was larger than most king-size beds, measuring two meters deep by four meters long. From that desk and the control board that occupied the left third of the top, he could access the thousands of miniature video relay systems and microphones hidden throughout the base.

Larson, the chief of security, stood slightly behind the Professor and to his left. From there he could work the monitor control board on the desk when the Professor asked him to.

Unlike Kleist who was built solidly, with broad shoulders and thick arms, Larson was tall, skinny,

and deceptively strong. He had short black hair
and deep black eyes. It seemed like he never
blinked, which unnerved many around him.

Like the Professor, Larson now stared at the
center four monitors, all presently showing different scenes from Sergeant Green's recent mission
into the alien sector. The monitors above the center four were focused on the Marine's current activities.

Kleist pointed at the bloody picture of Boone,
deserted in the alien section. With a few key
strokes on the inside right of the control board, he
focused the camera in close and sat forward in his
chair. Boone lay sprawled on the stone floor, the
head and upper chest of the alien warrior slightly
across her legs. Her hair hung out of the hole in
the back of her helmet and one alien arm and
claw still clung to her waist. There were no other
bugs in sight and nothing had disturbed the scene
since the retreat of the Marines. "Can we save the
body?"

Larson stared at the scene for a moment before
answering. "I'll have some of my men check, but I
doubt it. The idiot who killed the alien managed
to cover the woman's body in acid blood. I doubt
the armor could hold it all back."

Kleist nodded. "I hope you're not right, but I
suspect you might be. Check anyway. If the burns
are only superficial we could use it."

Larson turned away from the Professor and
softly gave instructions into his personal mike.

The Professor nodded in satisfaction, leaving
one screen on the woman's body so he could
watch when Larson's men got there.

His hand did a quick dance on the control

board, then he leaned back in his chair and ran both hands through his thinning hair, his gaze again intent on the four Marines as they half carried, half dragged the alien warrior toward the labs. He watched, following their progress through the corridors as the system automatically switched from hidden camera to camera until the four Marines had the warrior delivered to the dissection vat.

Then he leaned forward and punched another key, sending his voice into the lab. "Nice work, Sergeant Green. It looks like a fine specimen."

He paused for a moment until all four Marines were looking up at the one obvious camera in the corner of the lab above them. Then he said, "But I am distressed that you slaughtered the other one, however."

"He's distressed," Private Choi shouted. The Professor could see the private shaking and he smiled. Good. He had gotten to the kid.

The private pulled off his helmet, his red hair falling long over the back of his suit. "Kleist, you son of a bitch! I should—"

Green grabbed the private's arm and yanked him almost off his feet. Green was twice the size of Choi and just one arm was as big around as Choi's waist.

Kleist sat back in his chair watching, smiling. Sergeant Green was not one to be underestimated. Not only was he a big brute of a man, he understood very well the ruling systems here on Charon Base.

"Sir, I can explain," Sergeant Green started, but Choi yanked his arm away and stepped closer to the one obvious camera.

"Kleist," Choi said, "we could have all been killed in that ant farm of yours. Boone is dead. You understand? Dead!"

He yelled the words though the meaning of them started to choke him up. But he went on, "And all you can be distressed about is that we killed one of your bugs. I don't think you're playing with a full deck."

Kleist smiled and turned to Larson, who was also grinning.

"Sir," Sergeant Green started to say, stepping up beside Choi and shoving him roughly aside.

"Sergeant Green," Kleist said softly, but with enough force to make the sergeant stop. "I can appreciate the private's feelings, but I suggest he restrain himself before he says something he will regret. It was a successful mission. That will be all for the day."

Kleist punched the microphone off, then leaned back to observe what happened next. He could hear everything they were saying, even when whispered. This was going to be interesting.

"Kiss his big ass, why don't you?" Choi said, turning square on the sergeant. His face was almost as red as his hair and he was half crouched in an attack posture.

"Private!" Sergeant Green said sharply. "Do yourself a favor and rein it in."

Choi seemed to deflate slightly. His shoulders slumped and his gaze dropped to the floor.

The sergeant took a deep breath and let it out. "Look. I'm sorry about Boone, but there's a time and a place for everything. Here and now is *not* it. Understand?"

"Yeah, right," Choi said. He threw his helmet

across the room and it smashed into a wall, scattering files and making a lab table jump under the force of the impact.

Green put a firm hand on his shoulder and said softly, "The bugs aren't the only things you have to worry about around here. Now clam it up and hit the showers."

He waited until Choi had shrugged off his hand and started toward the door, then he turned to the other two members of the squad. "And that goes for both of you, too."

Professor Kleist laughed and leaned back in his chair. "How right you are, Sergeant. How right you are." He spun to face Larson. "It seems the stock needs some new breeding material, and Private Choi there just volunteered."

"It seems that he did," Larson said, smiling.

The Professor stood and slipped into his white lab coat. "I have work to do. This new warrior just may be the one. I'm close, so very close."

Captain Joyce Palmer pulled the yellow Harley-Davidson cap down firmly on her head and then strapped herself into the pilot's chair, buckling first the lap belt and then both shoulder straps. Deegan was already strapped in beside her, running diagnostic checks and preparing for docking. In front of them was the main control board for the shuttle and two windows looking out into the blackness of space. In the center between the windows was a large monitor, at the moment black and not in use.

Their passenger, Mr. Cray, looked tired and somewhat ruffled. He was strapped into one of

two passenger seats along the wall behind
Deegan. He wore pressed cloth pants, a dress
shirt unbuttoned at the neck, and a brown leather
jacket. She had nodded hello as she passed him in
the small cockpit area of the shuttle and he had
nodded back without a smile.

In the entire trip he hadn't said more than two
sentences to her. Deegan had talked his ear off
over the one dinner before cold sleep, but she
doubted if Cray had even said three words back.
Of course, Deegan didn't usually need much more
than three words to keep him going for hours.

"Nice shirt," she said to Deegan as she finished
her adjustments and slipped the headset over her
cap. It was a ritual they always went through right
before landing. Deegan always wore his lucky
Budweiser T-shirt with a faded picture of an ugly
dog on it. He said it had been his dad's. It had
been patched more times than she wanted to
think about and it still had holes all over it. But it
was his lucky T-shirt and he always wore it for
landings.

"I'm glad you like it," he said, smiling.

Behind them she heard Cray give a snort of disgust. That was good. At least he had some taste.
Her lucky landing clothes were far less obvious.
She just had on a white T-shirt, brown cloth
slacks, and a brown open vest. In the pocket of
the vest she had a picture of Cass and Drake. That
picture always rode against her chest and her
heart every takeoff or landing. It wasn't as obvious a good-luck charm as Deegan's shirt, but it
was her private one.

She adjusted the mike so it was just below her
lower lip, then nodded to Deegan and punched up

the transmit code. "Charon Base Flight Control. This is the transport vessel *Caliban* requesting landing clearance. Sending identification codes now." She punched in two more sequences on the console in front of her, then said, "Over."

Deegan pointed through the viewport at the bright light growing quickly in front of them. "There she is. Hell in space, our soon to be home away from home."

"Roger, *Caliban*." The deep voice of Hank, the flight controller, filled the control cabin. "Hangar twelve is clear and ready to receive you. Hope you had a safe trip, Joyce. Over."

Deegan glanced at Joyce and smiled, the glint in his eyes letting her know that *he knew* what had happened between Hank and her on the last run here. Or at least he thought he knew. Knowing the lack of privacy on Charon Base, he probably did. Every damn detail.

She ignored her copilot. "So far so good," she said. "Over."

"We're in the tube," Deegan said. "Normal to profile. Cutting thrusters." He was still smiling at her.

"All right," she said. "Let's tuck her in. And, Deegan—"

"Yes, boss?"

"Watch those corners this time."

Deegan laughed. "I missed that door by a good ten meters last time. This is a walk in the park."

She snorted. "When did you last see someone take eighty thousand tons of ugly metal for a stroll?"

He again laughed, but didn't take his eyes off his instruments. She sat back and watched as

Deegan, one of the best solo pilots working, took them in. Within thirty minutes he had the transport sitting snugly in the middle of the docking bay.

"Hangar deck secure. Outer doors closed. Deck pressurized," Hank's voice announced a moment after Deegan cut thrusters. "Crew and passengers please report to decontamination."

"Will do," Joyce said and cut the link. She had to admit she was looking forward to seeing Hank again. It seemed like it had been a long time, even though for her it had only been a little over a month real-time. But for Hank it actually had been a long time, a little over a year and a month. Maybe he was married by now or more likely no longer interested in her. She let the thought drop. No point in worrying about it. She'd find out soon enough.

She let Deegan, now wearing a cloth jacket over his tattered shirt, lead her and Cray out of the ship and down the ramp. They strode across the hangar deck in silence as service technicians swarmed around the transport.

The decontamination chamber was nothing more than a narrow spot in the main passage leading from the deck. As the three of them stepped inside, big metal doors ahead and behind them slid shut with a loud bang. She thought it would be much easier on the nerves to not have such loud doors. But at every base the decontamination doors slammed shut, a very annoying design feature.

A fine mist and bluish light filled the area. Joyce always thought the decontamination chamber smelled like apples, but Deegan said it was more like floor polish. They had argued about it a number of times. Again she smelled apples.

She turned slightly as they stood for the required thirty seconds so that she could see Cray better. He seemed to be used to the process. No trace of emotion crossed that cold face—at least none that she could see.

She, on the other hand, hated the procedure. She always felt naked in these chambers. Not only were they killing the unwanted microscopic bugs that might be hitching rides, but somewhere, behind some monitors, people she didn't know were looking her insides over very carefully for bigger bugs. Alien-type bugs. She was glad they did, but it still made her feel very exposed knowing someone—maybe even Hank—was looking at her every private part.

She again shook off the thought and turned to Cray. "So, what brings you to scenic Charon?"

"Apart from us, that is," Deegan said.

"Excuse me, Deegan, but I'm trying to have a conversation with a real human."

Cray smiled slightly and Joyce immediately liked him better. "Thanks for the interest, but it's classified." He turned and actually looked at her. "Need to know and all that."

"And we don't need to know?"

"Got it in one," Cray said, but his eyes told her it was nothing personal.

"Figures," Deegan said as the chamber doors banged open and they entered the carpeted area of the base. "Kleist has this place sewn up tighter than a frog's butt."

"Mr. Cray," Professor Kleist said as he rounded the corner ten meters in front of them, and Joyce instantly tightened. The Professor gave her the creeps. His cheeks seemed to always be flushed and his eyes felt more like animal eyes than human ones.

Two others followed the Professor and Joyce shuddered again as they came into sight. One was the Professor's main henchman, Larson, a tall, wiry man who was by far the nastiest human she had ever met. The other was the Professor's android secretary, Grace. Grace had short blond hair, a body only science could manufacture, and a smile that could freeze a waterfall. Joyce regarded all three with equal loathing. She'd never had a run-in with any of them, but she had heard enough stories.

"Speak of the devil," Joyce said softly as they continued toward the Professor.

"And he shall appear," Cray said, just as softly. A moment later he was smiling and shaking the Professor's hand as introductions were made.

"I trust you had a comfortable flight?" Kleist asked Cray.

"Yes," Cray said, glancing at Joyce. "It was most enlightening."

"Good, good. Glad to hear it." Kleist patted Cray on the back, then steered him away from the pilots and down the hall. "We must get to our business."

Joyce and Deegan stood and watched the Professor's party walk away. When they were far enough away Joyce said softly, "Hmm . . . he could be interesting."

"Who?" Deegan asked. "Kleist? Or the corporation suit?"

"None of your damn business," she said.

"Ha, you have a heart under all that ice after all."

"Yeah," Joyce said, "I do. It belonged to my last wise-ass copilot."

Deegan laughed as they followed the Professor and his group at a safe and sane distance into the human sections of the station.

In the silent quarters of the Marines, Sergeant Green slowly picked through Boone's locker. Choi was nowhere to be found and the others were at dinner. It was as good a time as any to finish up his most dreaded chore.

He glanced down the row of single, tightly made beds and green lockers. When they had arrived this room had been full. Full of life and energy. Full of his men.

Now only half of them were left. He had cleaned out over half his troop's personal effects and shipped them back to families on Earth. Half dead. How could that be?

And now he was doing another.

This was wrong. This was different than losing good men and women fighting an enemy. Here his soldiers had died at the hands of alien prisoners, solely for the benefits of Professor Kleist and Z.C.T. Corporation's research.

This wasn't war; this wasn't honorable death. This was just profit.

He picked up a photo Boone had of her friends. It was taken on a green lawn on Earth, with the Earth-orbit shuttle in the background, right before their departure on this mission. Boone's arm was around Choi and they were both beaming like the world was the nicest, safest place to be. Green supposed that together it had seemed that way then.

But now Boone was dead, rammed through by an alien and covered in acid blood. And Choi was alone.

Green shook his head. As they always said, the corps took everything you've got to give.

And then more.

Green dropped the photo on top of the few belongings Boone had left and closed the box. He picked it up and tucked it under his arm. Such a small box, so few things for a human to leave behind. He glanced around the room at the freshly made beds, the perfect order of the lockers. Alive or dead, he was proud of his men and of the Marines. It was all he knew.

It was his life and his soul..

Maybe the corps did take everything you had to give, but it was never in vain.

Never.

As long as someone remembered.

3

The Professor escorted Cray to the living quarters and left him to get settled in, taking with him the transmission disk Cray had brought from the Z.C.T. Corporation headquarters. The disk he had said was the only reason for his long trip. A very strange reason, indeed, to eat up fifteen months of a man's life.

Back in his office, behind breach-proof doors, the Professor gave only a slight glance at the screens in front of him, then settled into his chair and keyed the transmission disk with his thumbprint. A red light blinked for a moment, then reset to green on the disk cover.

The Professor nodded and inserted the disk in the play slot of the decoding imager. If nothing

else, this was going to be interesting. He knew a
great deal about Mr. Cray. A black belt in karate
and a spy with no equal. The list went on. Much
more information than Cray would want him to
know, he was sure. And everything that involved
Cray was always interesting.

The Professor leaned back, his fingers steepled
in front of his chin as the hologram shimmered
into place over the front edge of his desk. The image first relayed the standard corporation gold
and black logo, Z.C.T., with the "Z" and the "T"
overlaid over the "C." Following the logo after a
few seconds were the blocklike words "EYES ONLY:
PROFESSOR ERNST KLEIST FROM G. D. SQUAZA, CONTROL-
LER, RESEARCH AND DEVELOPMENT."

A moment later the words were replaced by the
image of the Professor's old friend, Gordy Squaza,
the second most powerful man in Z.C.T. Corporation, sitting behind his glass and chrome desk. Behind him a window overlooked the parklike
setting of the corporation headquarters. The Professor had looked out that window a number of
times while visiting Squaza and planning this base
and the Chimera Project. Even though the image
was smaller than life, the feeling of being at the
headquarters was very real and for just a moment
it gave the Professor a sinking feeling of home. He
shook the feeling, slightly angry at himself. This
was his home; this work was his life. He didn't
have time for wondering about Earth, or anyplace
else for that matter.

The Professor leaned toward the holographic
image of his old friend. "This is going to be fascinating."

"Hello, Ernst," Squaza said, then the image seemed to hold and flicker in repeat mode.

The Professor sat back and watched it, recognizing the standard coding for corporation holographic messages. If the wrong response or the wrong voiceprint was heard next, the disk would destroy itself.

"Hello yourself, Gordy," the Professor said carefully. His voice and words triggered a recognition sequence and the holographic image continued and sharpened. Again the Professor said softly, "I knew this was going to be good."

"Sorry about all the cloak-and-dagger business," Squaza said, his smile not totally hiding the seriousness in his brown eyes. "We have something of a situation here. Actually, 'situation' is a mild way of putting it. We have a mess here, plain and simple. And I thought you should be brought up to speed on the current events, even if this takes six months to reach you."

Actually, the Professor noted that the message had taken two days over seven months to get to him, but he didn't say a word, just listened and waited.

The image of Squaza grew until only his face filled the holographic image hovering over the Professor's desk.

Squaza took a deep breath and went on. "Ernst, your work on the Chimera Project is garnering unhealthy attention from certain quarters, including the Grant Corporation, B.M.I. Affairs, and a new Asian-Chinese consortium that's attempted to infiltrate Z.C.T. on a number of occasions. All have been fruitless efforts. Fruitless, that is, until now."

The image of Squaza pulled away and after a

moment Squaza stood and moved toward the window, obviously contemplating what to say next. The Professor just sat at his desk, his fingers again steepled in front of his chin, his gaze never leaving the image.

Finally Squaza turned and faced into the recorder directly. "Ernst, your last project update had problems. When we received the transmission, it had been intercepted and decoded."

"Really," the Professor said softly, without moving.

"It was a tidy job," Squaza said. "But close investigation showed that the data had not only been intercepted and decoded, but had been altered and infested with viral time bombs. Nasty things to say the least. They've cost us more time and energy than you can imagine. I'm not blaming you at all, so don't take what I am saying that way."

Squaza took a deep breath and then sat back down at his desk. "The point is that we can't be certain that this was the first time they have cracked our transmissions or the hundredth. We're having to deep-clean all our systems, which is a nightmare as you can imagine. And we don't know who or, for that matter, how they managed to crack our codes."

Again the camera focused in close on Squaza's face. "Ernst, we don't know if the problem is on our side or yours, but you must be extra careful. Your project is our corporation's highest priority, and until we discover the leak you are to cease transmissions to Earth until further notice. Security code Alpha C fifty-one."

The Professor smiled and sat back in his chair.

Now he was starting to understand. He watched as Squaza shuffled some papers on his desk, then looked back into the camera. "I know this will be hard on you and your fine staff, but it must be done. You can trust no one. Understand?"

"Oh, I understand all right," the Professor said softly. He didn't say out loud that that had been his belief from the start. He had never trusted anyone and had no plans to start now.

"We can't rely on our existing data because of the changes, so I have sent Cray to collect disk copies of everything you have for personal delivery to our labs."

The holo image suddenly switched from Squaza to a photo of Cray. Squaza's voice continued over the picture. "Ernst, I know what you are thinking, but relax. He's the best operative we've got. You have him to thank for that gel that reduces alien blood to the pH of water. He took that out from under the noses of the Grant Corporation. He also won for us the specs on the Taser Web launchers our troops use. There is no one else I'd trust on this mission, and I'm sure you'll give him the respect he deserves under the security code Alpha C fifty-one."

The Professor laughed softly and then said, "You can bet I will give him the best of everything. Just for you, Gordy."

For a moment longer the picture of Cray remained on the image, then Squaza's face reappeared. "Ernst, everyone around here is walking scared. Security is working on the problem of who broke the codes and how they just walked into our computers like they did. But as far as we can tell it has to be an inside job."

Squaza looked directly into the camera. "It's going to be a bad time, Ernst. As an old friend, I'm warning you to *protect* yourself as best you can and watch your back at all times."

"Always have, old friend," the Professor said softly. "And I hear you this time, too. Loud and clear."

The image panned back to show Squaza sitting at his desk again with the parklike corporation grounds through the window. "I envy you, Ernst, out there on your island in space. We could all do with a little extra security and isolation around here. Good luck."

The words "MESSAGE ENDS" filled the air above the desk and a moment later the disk popped out of the holo player.

Professor Kleist leaned back in his chair and stared at the empty air in front of him.

Then, after a long time, he laughed. Not loudly. Just a soft laugh at something that seemed really, really funny.

Private Choi was giving much more than he was taking in punishment from three of the Professor's elite security force. "Larson's goons" as most people called them. They always wore dark slacks, green shirts, and sneakers. Usually they carried small arms like pistols, but lately they had taken to wearing full shoulder belts full of ammunition and carrying Kramers, the newest in high-speed automatic rifles. Twenty-six shots in a clip and ten clips on a belt. On fully automatic fire setting, twenty-six shots from a Kramer could drill a hole through a half meter of solid concrete in a fraction of a second.

They were nasty weapons.

In the fight with Choi, however, the guards hadn't considered him dangerous enough to bring rifles and it had taken him only a moment to disarm all three of their handguns. Now Choi's white T-shirt was stained red with the blood of the three men who had jumped him. If Choi hadn't already been looking for some way to avenge Boone's death, he might have been caught by surprise.

But he wasn't and now he stood panting, his back to the corridor wall, his fists clenched in readiness. His right eye was quickly swelling shut and blood trickled down from his right ear, almost matching the color of his bright red hair. He could feel that he had broken some bones in his right hand, but he didn't really care. It felt good to be fighting humans again, not stupid bugs. And since it was the Professor who had ordered Boone to her death, he would certainly take it out on the Professor's security force with pleasure.

One blond-headed security man lay on his back in the center of the corridor, his head cracked and bleeding, his brown uniform rumpled and torn in two places. Choi doubted if he was still breathing and didn't care much one way or the other.

The other two remained standing, weaponless, one on each side of the hall from Choi. The one to Choi's right had blood streaming from a crushed nose making the front of his brown uniform appear almost black. The guy was looking pale and would be slow moving.

"Give it up, Choi," the other guy said, but didn't

make a move. Choi laughed to himself. The guy was smarter than he looked.

"Screw you," Choi said, his voice low and mean. "And your asshole Professor, too." With a quick faint toward the one who had spoken, Choi spun and connected with a hard left-footed kick to the already smashed nose of the guy on the right as he started forward.

He caught him with his arms at his sides and a surprised look on his face. Choi could hear the bones in the guy's face crack and splinter as his head snapped back. Blood spattered the walls and ceiling and with a loud scream the guard tumbled backward, ending up facedown against the wall. A pool of dark blood quickly formed under his head. He wasn't moving and Choi doubted he ever would again. No great loss.

Choi spun to face his last attacker. "Your turn."

The guy shook his head and was slowly backing away when two more security guards entered the narrow hall from a side corridor and moved in beside the last remaining goon. Choi recognized Bergren, Larson's second in command. In his hands he carried a Taser Web gun used to take down aliens.

"Now it's a fair fight again," Choi said. He wiped his hands on his pants and moved into the very center of the corridor, preventing any of them from flanking him.

"What's the problem?" Bergren asked, giving a quick glance at his two men on the floor.

"You sci-tech maggots aren't fit to lick Boone's boots," Choi said, his voice hard and calm. "And now she's dead and you're not. That pisses me off."

The guy who remained from the first round turned slightly to Bergren. "Larson said the Professor wanted us to give this insubordinate grunt the treatment, but we couldn't get near him. He fought like a mad dog."

"I am *mad*, you stupid ass." Choi made a fake lunging move at the men, and all three took a step back.

"Cowards," Choi said, shaking his head and laughing. "My Boone died for a scum professor and a bunch of cowards. I just don't think that's right, do you?"

"But she didn't die in vain," Bergren said. "Luckily the suit protected her beautiful skin and body from most of the acid so she could be *used* again."

Choi stood slowly from his fighter's couch, his mind trying to make sense of what Bergren had said. "Used? What—" But before he could say anything more Bergren raised the Taser Web and fired.

The web, with its numbing, stinging needles, covered Choi before he had a chance to react. He dropped to one knee, the needles working instantly, making the web feel as if it weighed a ton.

He managed to get his hands under the web, but before he could pull it off his legs gave out and he fell over on his back to the floor.

His mind shouted that he should struggle, but his muscles betrayed him and he lay there, bound by webs designed to hold and control aliens twenty times stronger.

Bergren turned to the man Choi left standing and pointed to the two on the floor. "See what you can do for Pavin and Thomas, there, if you can manage to get that right." Then Bergren motioned for the other man to help him as he leaned over Choi.

"I'll kill you," Choi somehow managed to spit out at Bergren as the room spun and he began to lose consciousness.

Bergren laughed. "Dream on, dog boy. I'm the least of your problems. When you see what comes next you'll be begging me to save your stupid hide."

And the last thing Choi heard as the blackness overwhelmed him was Bergren's laughter.

Joyce sat up straight and took a deep breath, doing the best she could to pull oxygen into her lungs. Sweat ran off her forehead and into her eyes and an intense heat seemed to radiate from every pore of her body. She could heat half the base from what was pouring off her.

"I can die happy now," she said, her voice no more than a whisper. She let her upper body sag onto Hank's chest and then she rolled to the right and off of his panting, sweaty body. She lay on the rumpled and damp sheets staring up at the tiled ceiling of Hank's bedroom, just letting the warmth of the moment flow into her memory for the next time she woke from cold sleep.

"You all right?" he asked. His hand eased over and touched her arm.

She laughed. "A lot better than I ever expected to be this far from Earth." She took a deep shuddering breath and forced herself onto her side, her head propped in one hand.

Then she looked at him. Really looked at him.

His face was flushed, which gave him a healthy look seldom seen on the pale deep-space workers. He had a full head of dark brown hair that at the moment was slicked back off his forehead with sweat. His chest was well muscled and it was clear he worked out with weights regularly. She had always liked the feel and the look of his white skin against her black. It was as if there were a line drawn between them that left her feeling just a little safer. A line that wouldn't allow him, or anyone else, all the way inside her defenses.

Yet at times like these she was glad he was with her and she didn't want to exclude him in any way.

She ran her hand over his mostly hairless chest. "How about you?"

"Very, very glad you came back."

"Thought I was gone for good, huh?" She let her finger trace a line in the sweat on his arm.

"I figured after that last time you'd stay on Earth, or get runs closer in, and I'd never see you again."

"Can't say as I didn't think about it. But the money out here for this one last trip will let me finish raising the kids the way they need to be raised."

He nodded and took a deep breath. Not looking at her he said, "You just be careful while you're here." Suddenly his voice had a sad and very serious edge to it.

"Why?" she asked. "Are things getting worse?"

He turned and looked at her for a moment and she could tell that she might have gone too far with that question. His eyes were almost shouting "No!"

With just a slight hesitation he laughed. "Nope, just about the same as always around here, from what I can tell. Of course, I don't pay that much attention." He patted her slick thigh and let his hand drift upward into her damp crotch for a moment. Then smiling, he said, "How about taking a long hot shower with me?"

She gave his hand a quick squeeze with her legs and beat him off the bed. "Only if we can start the water off cool for a few minutes."

"Deal."

They made small talk for the few minutes it took them to get into the shower and then after they both were standing naked together under the spray, Hank whispered in her ear, "You've got to be really, really careful. The Professor and his goon, Larson, have cameras and bugs everywhere. Not only the ones you can see, but many more you can't."

Joyce recoiled slightly at the thought of Larson and the Professor watching as she and Hank made love. Could he have listened to their every word, their every sound of passion?

Hank spun her around slowly, grabbed the soap, and started working slowly up and down her back. It felt wonderful, easing the sudden tension the thoughts of the Professor had brought to her shoulders.

"It's the truth," he said softly in her ear. "You have a great ass," he said more loudly as he ran the soap over her cheeks and then down the backs of her legs.

On the one hand it felt wonderful, and on the other she couldn't shake the possibility that someone was watching. Even with the soap and the hot water, the very thought made her feel dirty.

She turned around and pulled Hank into a hug, as if they were slow-dancing. In a whisper she asked, "What's been happening around here?"

Hank soaped her back as he answered. "Two years ago there were over fifteen hundred people—civilians, scientists, and just simple hired hands—on this station, including forty Marines. I bet if we were to do a total now it wouldn't break fourteen hundred. And there's only twenty Marines left. People just keep disappearing. Some are accidents. Some without reason or explanation. And the Marines keep getting killed on missions into the hive area."

"You're kidding," she whispered and he shook his head no. He wasn't kidding, but she didn't want to let herself believe what he was saying. That many people disappearing on a closed station like this wasn't possible.

"I wish I were kidding," Hank whispered, turning her slowly around so that her back was under the warm spray. "The Professor has become like an evil god around here and his security force is much more powerful than the Marines, numbering over a hundred men the last time I heard."

"A hundred men out of fourteen hundred." That seemed like overkill to her. Why would the Professor need that many security men on a closed, isolated station in deep space? It simply made no sense.

"That's right," Hank said. "Anyone who stands up against the Professor or Larson, or even Bergren, disappears very shortly. And anyone who even questions what happened does the same."

Joyce shook her head. "There's got to be some-one to investigate this, stop it."

Hank didn't say anything for a moment, just let-ting the water run down her back and shoulders. Finally he asked, "Did anyone back on Earth or at Z.C.T. headquarters mention the name of the pro-ject being worked on here?"

Joyce again shook her head. "Nothing. I wasn't even allowed to mention that I was leaving Earth's system until we were in deep space and ready for cold sleep. I didn't even know exactly that I was coming back here until we were well away from Earth. I just knew it was a deep-space mission. Then it turned out I was just to bring one man here and wait for his return. Very, very secret."

"That's the problem," Hank said. "We're so damn far from Earth that there just isn't anything we can do about the missing people. What few ships do come and go with supplies are monitored so tightly for security reasons that nothing leaves here without Larson and the Professor knowing."

"And Z.C.T. is behind him?" Joyce asked, know-ing the answer to her obvious question.

"Totally."

They stood under the water, letting it pound their bodies without breaking into their thoughts.

"So how do we stop him?"

Hank shook his head. "*We* don't. *We* get out of this shower before we turn into prunes, go back to those sweat-stained sheets, and get some sleep. Then in the morning you make love to me or I make love to you, depending on who wakes up first."

"And we just let the Professor go on being God?"

Hank turned off the water and grabbed towels for both of them. "You got it." He hesitated for a moment, then said in a normal voice, "I think they're still delivering pizza from the west kitchen. Should I call for one?"

Joyce nodded and then studied the soft golden towel in her hands for a moment before moving to dry her hair. Hank was right. She had no stake in this. Better to just get back to Earth and then report it.

Larson watched Joyce towel off and move into Hank's bedroom before he turned and faced the Professor. "You think she's going to be a problem?"

Kleist watched on the center monitor as she climbed into bed and huddled next to the flight controller. "I'm sure she is. No telling what Cray told her on the way out here, and since we're going to keep her passenger for a time, she might find out things on her own."

"You want me to take care of her?" Larson asked. "I'd be glad to do it."

"I know you would," the Professor said, then shook his head. "No. We may need her and her ship. Let's just keep a close watch on her until that time comes."

Larson nodded, and with one last glance at the naked couple on one of the many screens that filled the wall, he moved toward the door. It would be his pleasure to watch her closely.

Very closely indeed.

4

Choi slowly fought his way back to consciousness, his first thought of Boone. He had always loved the way she looked after working out, her face covered in a fine sheen of sweat, her thin, soaked T-shirt stretched almost invisible by her muscles and chest. Her small brown nipples always poked through her shirt like they were calling for attention, and he tried to give them as much as she would let him.

But most of all he loved the way she smelled after exercising. An earthy, wet-clay sort of smell that turned him on like nothing else ever could. He would run his face across her sweaty arms or back or shoulders burying himself against her, never wanting to let go. Choi had been lucky that

Boone liked his love of her smell. They had made love after almost every workout. Boone called it her reward.

But Choi knew secretly it was much more his reward.

In his mind he could see her face—her small nose, her bright eyes—as if they were in front of him now. She smiled at him, called to him, and then the alien jaws cut through her face, smashing her smile, cutting off her call. The alien's jaws drooled her blood, leering at him, laughing at his inability to help her. He fought to go to her, but something held him back.

The alien's jaws sliced through her face and her blood was everywhere.

She was dead.

Overwhelming sadness caught him like a hard blow to the stomach. Boone was dead. He had watched her die, unable to move fast enough to save her. He wanted to die, too. Join her wherever she was now.

He moaned and tried to roll over, but something held him like a heavy, wet blanket. He could barely feel his legs and arms and his head felt thick, like he had a bad hangover. He struggled to remember where he was, what he had been doing that would cause this, but the nightmare of her face exploding in front of him kept filling his vision and he couldn't shake it.

"End of the line, dog boy," a voice said from above. Choi's mind cleared a little and the smell of rotten eggs filled his senses like a hammer pounding his thick skull. Oh, Jesus Christ Almighty! He was in the alien sector. What the hell was going on? He fought to open his eyes to blurry, faint

light. Was Boone really dead? Had that all been a
bad dream? Had he gotten hurt on the last mission instead?

"Nice nap?" the voice said and a rough hand
pulled Choi into a sitting position with his back to
the wall.

Choi shook his head carefully and took a few
deep breaths of the humid, rancid air. He knew
that voice. "Bergren?"

"Nice to have you back with us," Bergren said.
He was standing over Choi with a pistol in one
hand. "That was quite a job you did on my men."

Choi's hands quickly fought to pull some of the
remaining Taser Webs from his legs and body. He
blinked and his gaze finally focused on Bergren,
then he glanced around. They were in the alien
section all right, just inside the west airlock. Slime
formations covered some of the walls and the
smell was so thick the air seemed to have texture
to it.

It looked as if they were alone. None of the
Professor's other men were in sight at least.

"Bergren," Choi said, pulling off more webs and
flexing his legs, "you're gonna die."

Bergren laughed, but his pistol never wavered.
"I don't think so. You Marines have just pushed
the Professor a little too far. Someone's gotta slap
you down."

"Yeah, and you're elected, right?" Choi almost
had the webs off his legs and was struggling to
stand. He would show this two-bit jerk that no
one got away with shooting him with a Taser like
he was some damn bug.

Bergren laughed again. "Yeah, lucky me. I get to
help you Marines know your place in the Profes-

sor's larger plan. Only, I'm afraid, it's just a little too late for you to learn much from the lesson."

Bergren's gun moved slightly lower and the sound of a shot echoed through the stone tunnels and caverns.

For just a moment Choi thought Bergren had missed him. He started to move, but then, as if in slow motion, his own blood splattered his face and the pain from his leg almost blacked him out.

He twisted around and grabbed his leg, focusing on releasing the pain like he and Boone had learned in basic. Don't think about the pain. Just react.

Don't think about the pain.

Just react.

He could almost hear Boone's voice repeating that with him, over and over.

Don't think.

React.

"You—you bastard!" Choi pulled his good leg underneath him and pushed off, lunging for Bergren.

Bergren quickly stepped back a few steps and the lunge fell short, leaving Choi to fall twisting on the hard floor, in even more pain than before as his wounded leg banged the hard surface.

"You were a dead mother the minute you smeared that damn bug," Bergren said, standing just out of Choi's reach. "The Professor doesn't like his pets being hurt."

Choi fought the blackness back. Don't think about the pain. Just react.

Don't think about the pain. Just react.

Quickly he dragged himself back over to the stone wall and forced himself to stand. For a moment the dizziness and the pain held him down, but he fought through it and finally gained his feet.

Bergren was walking quickly toward the airlock to the human quarters.

"Wait!" Choi shouted, glancing around the damp, smelly corridor. For the first time it dawned on him what Bergren was doing. Choi started to jump one-legged for the airlock, but the drugs from the Taser and the shock of his wound made him too weak. He fell face-first on the floor, his right hand searching for the small knife in the boot holster on his injured leg. It was slick, covered in his own blood. He palmed it and again shouted for Bergren to wait.

Bergren opened the airlock and stood just inside the alien section framed by the light from the corridor beyond.

Choi got a burst of fresh air, but it was smothered by the stench and humid thickness of the alien caverns and that hated smell of rotten eggs.

With his hand still on the airlock button, Bergren glanced back at Choi. "I'd love to make this clean for you, but it's not worth my life. Crossing the Professor is never a wise move, but I suppose you understand that now. Right?"

Choi pulled himself hand over hand toward the airlock, dragging his useless leg behind him, ignoring the pain and the weakness.

Just react.

Just react, he repeated, over and over. Don't think. Just react.

Panic blurred his thoughts, but his training won out and he kept moving, pushing to escape.

Pushing to get closer to that door.

Bergren watched for a moment, then shrugged like it didn't make any difference. "I've got to hand it to you, Choi, you are one tough mother. Maybe you'll be lucky." He started to step through the door. "Maybe you'll bleed to death before implantation."

Without thinking or even aiming Choi swung up into a sitting position and sent the knife in a practiced underhand flick toward Bergren.

The thick sound of the blade burying itself in Bergren's chest filled Choi's ears with pleasure.

Bergren, one hand on the knife, a look of total shock and dismay on his face, staggered against the door frame.

Choi crawled toward the open door as fast as he could.

Bergren looked down at the knife, then back at Choi as his eyes glazed over and he toppled into the alien sector. Behind him the airlock slid closed with a resounding clang that reverberated down the dark corridors.

"No!" Choi shouted.

But his words only echoed through the hot, dark corridors. He was alone where no man dared to be alone. Behind him he heard a rustling noise that quickly grew to fill the small stone cavern.

Don't think. Ignore the pain. Just react.

He pushed Bergren's body aside and stretched up for the button on the airlock, pounding it hard over and over again.

Nothing. It was closed and it wasn't going to open. He could tell.

He turned, pushed himself up with his arms, got his good leg underneath his butt, and stood. Insistently he punched the open button, but the door wasn't moving. He tried to yank it open with brute strength, but it didn't even budge. He was trapped.

He almost toppled over as he reached down and pulled his knife out of Bergren's chest, wiping the blood on Bergren's shirt. "At least you went with me," he said.

He stood and leaned lightly against the airlock door. "Boone," he said intently to the air around him. "I ain't going down without a fight. You're going to be proud of me." He pulled another knife out of his other boot and stood facing the darkness.

There was a rustling in the shadows and the smell grew stronger.

Choi shouted into the dark caverns, "Come and get me, you Bitch!"

And almost before he had time to blink, she did.

The Professor nodded and turned from the wall of monitors to face Larson. "Too bad about your man Bergren, but this only proves he was careless and soft. Have your men retrieve his body. I can use it."

Larson nodded, still staring at the screen and the body of his second in command.

"Also," Kleist said, "you can expect trouble from Sergeant Green."

Larson forced himself to look at the Professor. "Not if he doesn't find out."

"Oh, he'll know," the Professor said. "And please make sure that he does. Do you understand?"

Larson just nodded, glancing back to the picture of Bergren's body. The alien had killed the struggling Choi by breaking his back like a dry stick. Blood rolled out of Choi's mouth as the alien pulled him out of the range of the camera and toward the center of the hive.

"Any movement from our shuttle pilot and her boyfriend?"

"She was asleep, last time I checked," Larson said. "I have someone monitoring her round-the-clock. Hank's on duty. They have a date for dinner after he gets off."

The Professor turned back to face the screen and sat unmoving, thinking. Every detail seemed to be in place. It would be another thirty hours before he knew if his latest experiment was going to succeed. So many failures, so many close calls. But he had a feeling this would be the one and thirty hours from now he would know.

"It seems," the Professor said, "that I have a little time to kill. Where is our Mr. Cray?"

Larson leaned over the edge of the desk and punched up a view in the center screen, then nodded toward it. "In his quarters, just sitting on his bed. From what I can tell he hasn't moved in two hours. That guy's a strange bird."

The Professor studied the solid frame of his guest. For being one of the best spies, he certainly didn't look much like one, whatever a spy was supposed to look like. Maybe it would be interesting to bait the guy a little, give him just a little rope. See how good he really was.

"Have Grace bring our guest to the labs. I might as well show him around." The Professor stood and took his lab coat off its hook beside the door.

He put the coat on and was about to leave when a soft bell chimed. Larson punched a key on the control board on the Professor's desk and listened for a moment, then clicked it off and looked up at the Professor. "Just our shuttle pilot. She's awake and headed for the lounge."

The Professor nodded. "I'm not sure exactly why I don't like that woman, but I just don't. I can sense the trouble she's going to bring."

"I'll watch her," Larson said.

"Of that I have no doubt," the Professor said.

As the door clicked closed behind Kleist, Larson dropped into the Professor's big padded chair. With a quick series of keystrokes he cleared the images of Bergren from the center screens.

Then, on three screens and from three different angles, he followed Joyce Palmer into the main lounge.

He loved to watch her.

In just the last day he knew most of her habits, where the scar on her right leg was, and what she did in the bathroom when she brushed her teeth. Someday he might even catch her alone and if the Professor gave him permission she'd find out she had a really true admirer.

The cool, clear taste of Mountain Crystal cut the fog from Joyce's mind and she nodded to the bartender, indicating her drink. "Nice, Jonathan. Real nice."

He smiled back at her, patted the bar lightly twice, and moved off to help the waitress at the end of the counter. Joyce took another sip, letting the cold, clear liquid fill her mouth as she settled into the high-backed bar stool. Being with Hank had been wonderful, almost better than it should have been, but she couldn't—or maybe it was "shouldn't"—let herself care too much for him. She would be leaving within the week, maybe within the day, to go back to Earth and her children, never to see him again. Getting too attached would be just plain stupid.

Good sex. That was all it could be.

Ever.

Of course, she didn't want to believe that deep down. There was just something between her and Hank that she hadn't felt in years, and it felt good. Really good.

She took another sip of the Mountain Crystal and tried to force her thoughts from Hank. She glanced around the bar, noting that there were only a dozen people in the room, most sitting together in one corner laughing and talking. This place was officially called the East Lounge, but many called it the "Jungle" because of all the plants. Vines ran along dividers between the cloth booths and the wooden tables in the middle of the room were separated by small trees in pots and large fernlike bushes. The carpet was a deep brown, the walls oak and the ceiling low. The lighting was spotlights, mostly aimed at the plants. The place always felt warm, almost cozy, and it was one of her favorite places on the base.

She studied the large group, wondering if there was anyone there she knew. And that thought reminded her that besides Hank she had other friends here on the base who would be mad at her if she didn't say hello real soon. She'd already left a message for Jerry, her and her husband's best friend. She hadn't heard back from him yet, which wasn't like him. Maybe she would give him a quick call while waiting for Hank to get off duty and have him join her and Hank for dinner. She was sure Hank wouldn't mind. He could have her alone later in the evening all he wanted.

"Jonathan," she said, waving her drink at the tall, slim bartender who stood talking with three men in white lab coats near the end of the bar. He wore tight black slacks and an open-necked shirt and was without a doubt the best-looking bartender she had ever seen.

He smiled and motioned that he would be right there. She took a long, slow drink and almost before she had the glass back on the bar Jonathan had another in front of her.

"That was fast," she said.

He laughed softly, his voice deep and rich. "That's what they pay me for."

"Jonathan," she said, "have you seen Jerry around lately? I left him a message right after I arrived, but haven't heard from him yet. That's not like him at all."

The bright, happy look on Jonathan's face slipped into a frown and his gaze dropped to something under the bar near his feet. He half choked on something, then said, "Guess you didn't hear?"

"Hear what?" It felt like the bottom of her stomach had dropped out.

Jonathan hesitated, not looking at her. Then he glanced up and blurted, "Jerry was killed in an airlock accident two months ago."

Hank's words about people disappearing, people getting killed for no reason, filled her mind like an echo chamber.

But not Jerry. Jonathan had it wrong.

She glanced up at the sad look on Jonathan's face.

He reached out but didn't touch her. "I'm sorry, Joyce."

Her mind wouldn't let Jonathan's words in. That couldn't happen to Jerry. He'd never die in an airlock accident. Never. He was too damn good a spacer for that. She started to get angry and was about to yell at Jonathan for pulling such a nasty trick, when she looked into his eyes and saw it was the truth.

Jerry was dead.

The realization overwhelmed her and she fought to keep control. She felt dizzy and the room blurred.

She must have been staring at her drink, not moving, because the next thing she knew Jonathan had a hand on hers and was squeezing it.

"I thought you would have heard."

She shook her head slowly, fighting to keep the tears from her eyes. God damn it all to hell, not Jerry.

Jerry was always there. Always. For the kids' birthday parties, sometimes to just baby-sit for them.

"Just a second," Jonathan said. "I'll get you a napkin."

She remained motionless, the cold glass of Crystal gripped tightly in her hand, fighting back any sign of tears and remembering Jerry. Remembering his bright, smiling face, his quick sense of

humor, his stupid dirty jokes that still made her
laugh.

She remembered all the nights she, Danny, and
Jerry had drunk and laughed together, most of
them ending with Jerry passed out on the couch.
She remembered all the missions they had been on
together during the invasion. Jerry had been there
for her when Danny was killed, had helped with his
funeral, had hugged her and let her cry.

And she had tried to be there for him at the
same time. Danny, after all, had been his best
friend. Together they had mourned for Danny and
Jerry had become almost a second father for the
kids before he was shipped out here. He had been
due back on Earth in two years to retire and just
fish and work in his bike shop.

Now he'd never get the chance.

Jonathan came up from digging under the bar
and quickly moved back in front of her. He
slipped a wadded-up napkin into her free hand.
"Here. Use this."

She nodded her thanks and dabbed her eyes
with the napkin. As she did so she noticed there
was something hard in the napkin. She was about
to stop and unwrap it when Jonathan put his hand
over hers.

She looked up into his dark, worried eyes. She
could see concern in them for her, but also fear.
Fear in his eyes and in the way he gripped her
hand, forcing her to hold tightly whatever was inside.

"I'm really sorry about Jerry," he said. "He was
a good guy. He didn't deserve to die."

She only nodded again, not trusting herself to
say anything.

"As a bartender, I'm pretty good at giving advice," he said, holding her gaze solid in his. "You might want to go someplace private, like your *ship*, and really just let go. Cry all you want. Might do you some good."

As he said the word "ship" he squeezed her hand and the message was clear. Again Hank's words about the Professor being able to see anything came flowing back to her, cutting through the anger and the grief, making her think cold hard thoughts.

"Thanks," she said, her voice sounding odd to her. "That's a good idea. I think I will."

She fumbled around in her pockets for a moment with one hand, not sure what she was looking for. Finally it dawned on her and she said, "What do I owe you for the drinks?"

Jonathan let go of her hand and waved. "Don't worry about it. Just take care of yourself."

She caught the double meaning in that last sentence, too. "Thanks," she said. She slid off the bar stool and headed slowly for the door, wiping away the tears and anger. She was real good at taking care of herself. If somehow the Professor was responsible for Jerry's death, she would take care of that, too.

But first she would see what Jonathan had given her. She couldn't imagine what it might be. But whatever it was, one thing had come through her anger and grief very clearly. He had been risking a great deal doing so.

Could things on this station really be that bad?

Twenty minutes later while sitting in the pilot's chair of her ship, she suddenly realized just how bad things on Charon Base really were.

* * *

The Professor stood just inside the lab door admiring the bustle of activity going on in the huge white room. Twenty or so lab techs in white coats sat or stood at monitors or moved quickly and with reason from one place to another, doing their jobs. He had some of the best scientists in all humanity working with him, right here in this room.

The room itself was almost a pure white and always scrubbed perfectly clean, yet to him it felt warm and friendly. Of all the places on the station, this was the area he was proudest of. He could spend days and nights in here, without the problems of the station and the outside world—or corporation politics—bothering him. His duty in this room was to the greater good of humanity and he knew that without a doubt.

The door behind him slid silently open and Grace escorted his visitor in. Cray was wearing tan slacks and a tan dress shirt with the sleeves casually rolled up. The colors stood out in sharp contrast to the bright white lab coats of everyone else.

The Professor noted that Cray's gaze took in the room quickly yet carefully, in a left-to-right scan. The Professor had no doubt that if Cray was to turn around and leave immediately, he would still be able to tell someone exactly what the room looked like and probably identify most of the machines in use. He was rumored to be good enough to even give descriptions of the twenty white-coated techs. Too bad there wasn't a way to test that theory.

"Welcome, Mr. Cray," the Professor said while

nodding to Grace that she was excused. "I thought you might like a little tour of my world."

Cray smiled and nodded. "I'd enjoy it a great deal."

The Professor laughed softly. "Wonderful. Follow me."

He led the way across the large, high-ceilinged white room. Today the Professor noted a slight smell of alien blood mixed with the cleaning solution smell. Not unusual, considering the work they did here.

As they moved through the room the Professor nodded to different workers at computer consoles. There was never a time that the main stations in this room were left untended.

The Professor led Cray over to a glass wall and stopped.

"The main dissection tank," the Professor said, indicating the clear, liquid-filled tank, itself the size of a good room. Three human figures in what appeared to be deep-space gear were carefully working over the remains of a large alien floating in the center.

"How do they avoid the acid blood?" Cray asked, taking a step closer to the glass and intently watching the work.

"I adapted the gel that I understand you acquired for the company into an effective dissection medium. This has enabled me to extensively analyze and catalogue the alien's morphology."

"Ingenious," Cray said.

"I agree," the Professor said, and then laughed at his own half joke. "Although I discovered more about function and alien physiology than anyone ever has before, it was at the molecular level that

I made the most startling find. The one the corporation gave me a blank check to pursue."

"The DNA Reflex?"

The Professor nodded, not exactly happy that Cray had that level of knowledge before he arrived. Now he was starting to understand exactly why Cray was here.

To Cray, with a nod of approval, the Professor said, "You've done your research, I see. Yes, tests show that an adult alien exhibits certain physical characteristics inherited from its host. We call it the DNA Reflex."

"So to change future generations of aliens, you give them different hosts."

Kleist nodded, again impressed. "That's exactly what we're doing here. Let me show you."

The Professor led the way down the hall and into a second large white room, two sides of which were walled with glass tanks. Behind the thick glass floated what looked to be human bodies. The Professor noted that his guest stopped suddenly, almost in shock. Good. Cray hadn't known about this aspect of the work.

The hairless, white bodies seemed to hand upright, naked, suspended in a clear fluid, bubbles drifting around them to the surface. Hoses ran from the backs of their necks, their heart areas, and their groins into the wall below and in front of their feet. A control panel monitored each body's functions and a white-coated technician was in charge of the monitoring stations, moving from one to the next, slowly and systematically, never stopping.

Every one of the naked forms hanging in suspension had a face-hugger alien on his face.

"You like my dummies?" the Professor asked after a moment.

"Dummies?" Cray asked, not taking his eyes off the human forms floating beyond the two glass walls.

"Dummies," the Professor said, closely watching Cray's expression as he studied the bodies. "That's what I call them. I cloned body tissue designed to mimic living matter to trick the alien implantation process. Yes, the aliens have inspired many new commodities."

"Amazing," Cray said as he turned and looked at the Professor. "I had no idea cloning had gone so far."

"It is amazing, isn't it?" He gave Cray a large smile, then indicated a door to the right. "Let me show you something else."

He led Mr. Cray out of the lab and into an area labeled "RESTRICTED" in bright red letters. As they walked their footsteps echoed off the smooth concrete walls.

"Imagine, Mr. Cray," the Professor said, "what might be the results if these creatures, these killing machines, could be bioengineered to become man's tool instead of his adversary?"

"Consumer biologicals?"

"Exactly," Kleist said, stopping in front of an airlock. A huge warning sign over it read: ALIEN SECTOR. DO NOT ENTER.

As he fumbled in his pocket, he went on, "I have removed the alien's innate hostility by splicing their DNA with that of more passive, less predatory creatures. I got the best results with sheep, lamas, and even some cattle. Of course, there were a few setbacks. There always are."

"The old adage about omelets and breaking eggs?" Cray said.

"Exactly," the Professor said. "All progress has its price. A necessary attitude, I think you'll agree. Logic and truth leave little room for moral posturing."

"I suppose," Cray said. "So from the way you sound I can assume you have had some success?"

The Professor smiled, pleased. He pulled a small instrument from his pocket, then turned to the wall in front of the airlock and started keying a command sequence into the control panel. "I'll show you some of my progress. It is quite extraordinary, if I do say so myself."

He finished keying his commands into the door panel, then turned to face Cray. "However, I admit I have yet to produce the equivalent of a queen. Royal jelly alone doesn't prove to be enough."

The airlock slid open with a clang.

Hot, stinking air hit them both and the Professor took a deep breath, relishing the odor as if his mother were baking his favorite pie.

Cray, on the other hand, choked and seemed on the verge of throwing up. Most humans hated the smell of aliens, but the Professor loved it. That wonderful smell signified his work.

He was making history.

"We're going in there?" Cray said, looking into the dark, slime-covered corridor ahead, obviously not happy with the thought.

The Professor laughed softly. "It's good to respect your fears, but don't let them rule you. Any good soldier should know that. And that's what we are, isn't it? Soldiers in the war against the aliens?"

"I suppose you might call us that," Cray said as he took a shallow, shuddering breath and hesitantly followed the Professor into the dimly lit corridor.

"Stay close to me," Kleist said. "No matter what happens, make no sudden noises or movement."

"Don't worry," Cray said.

The Professor raised the small device he had fished out of the pocket of his lab coat. It looked like a toilet paper tube, only with a few buttons on top.

"Interesting device, this." He held it up for a moment, but Cray seemed more intent on watching the shadows and the slime-covered walls where aliens had formed stringy, slick shapes and dark round pockets.

"I stumbled on its potential quite by accident," the Professor went on. "It somehow disrupts the impulses of what passes for the alien central nervous system. I've devised a larger version for securing wild specimens for study called a Sound Cannon by the Marines. This small one works more like a dog whistle."

He pointed it down the hall and pulled the trigger. It seemed that nothing happened, but he could feel the device in his hand humming.

A slight rustling started in the dark shadows down the corridor, like a den of snakes being disturbed on a hot summer day.

"Down there," Cray said, his voice a loud, insistent whisper.

"Keep calm," the Professor said. "They're coming." He continued to hold the trigger down until the black shadows at the end of the hall separated and became clear alien forms. Then he clicked it off and put the tube in his pocket.

The overpowering stench grew stronger and Cray took a step back toward the open airlock.

The Professor moved forward.

"Come on," the Professor said, talking to the forms in front of him, forgetting Cray and the open door behind him. "Don't be scared. It's only me."

Cray had backed step by step to the open door and stood watching, his mouth open in shock.

Two small aliens separated from the shadows and moved toward the Professor.

"Come to Daddy," the Professor said.

Both aliens crawled on the floor in front of Kleist like slaves in front of a master until the Professor finally reached down and stroked the hard shells on the back of their heads.

"There my good children," the Professor said softly, over and over. "There my good children."

5

Grace, the Professor's android secretary, walked silently up to where the Professor sat in the large white lab, intently studying his latest experiment on the computer monitor. Shoulders hunched, his gaze intent on the image of the alien on the screen, he seemed to be oblivious to all the other work going on around him. Grace stood silently behind him, waiting for him to acknowledge her. Everyone knew not to disturb the Professor until he wanted to be disturbed. And he had the uncanny ability to know who was behind him at any given moment.

After a full two minutes he finally said, without looking up, "Only ten more hours, Grace. Did you know that?"

"Yes, sir, I did."

"Ten more hours until I finally succeed. Ten more lousy hours until the course of human history is changed forever."

"Yes, sir," Grace said. "Ten more hours."

The Professor sighed and pushed his chair back from the computer monitor. "Now why should I hope to get a reaction from an android, especially when it comes to helping humanity? I must be losing touch with reality." He shook his head, half laughing at himself. "What did you need to report, Grace?"

"You told me you wanted to know when the possible subject is on the move. He is on the move now."

"Wonderful timing," the Professor said, clapping his hands and standing quickly. "Inform Larson that I would like him to meet me in the lower storage area. We might as well give our guest a personal welcome, wouldn't you say?"

"If that is what you want," Grace said.

The Professor looked at Grace, then sighed. "Yes. That's what I want. Get Larson."

He walked away shaking his head.

Grace smiled at his back. She loved doing that to him.

It took over two thousand convicts fifty years to hack the thousands of kilometers of tunnels known as Charon Base out of the cold hard rock. Over two thousand men who dug their own graves as they went along. All but a very few of those convicts still remained in the tunnels and caverns, their mummified remains filling the sleeping bunks carved into the ice-cold stone walls.

Andy Carrier had learned that the bodies were still there two months earlier over a poker game. The guy who told him had claimed to have helped in the original conversion of the base from a prison camp to a research facility and had seen dozens of convicts' bodies.

Two days later Andy had started searching, mostly on his days off from the kitchens, exploring the tunnels with a stolen oxygen mask. He would sneak through an old air vent into the unoccupied sections of the station, the areas not converted to the luxury needed by the Professor and his workers, or the walled-off and sealed sections of the alien hive. Thousands of kilometers of tunnels and caverns, carved out of solid rock simply for the purpose of keeping convicts busy and shortening their lives in the process.

And Andy wanted to explore it all.

In the black, cold tunnels Andy Carrier looked for the bodies of the dead.

Andy Carrier was a grave robber, a sideline that could turn the strongest stomach, but Andy was a practical man. Working the kitchen had given him a healthy disregard for dead meat. Besides, he figured the convicts didn't need the rings and gold teeth they took to their graves. They were dead. He wasn't.

And his "hobby," as he liked to call it, had turned out to be fairly simple and very, very profitable. Most of the lower tunnels had been carved in a clear pattern that made searching easy. Unlike the larger caverns in the upper areas, two levels below the human section the tunnels were in

mostly square patterns in the horizontal directions
with vertical shafts cutting up one side wall of
each tunnel intersection.

These intersections were usually no bigger than
a large living room, with four black doors—one
on each wall—and a large hole in both the floor
and ceiling near one wall. If you left an intersection and then kept turning left every time you
came to a new tunnel, you would find yourself
back where you started. The distance between the
tunnel intersections sometimes varied from as little as fifty meters to as much as two hundred meters.

The tunnels never seemed to be exactly
straight, but yet seemed to go in a fairly uniform
direction. And the tunnels varied from normally
wide enough for two people to walk side by side
on the flat floor without ducking to large caverns
with stone tables and bunks carved into the walls.

It was those larger caverns that Andy searched
for.

Today, the shift in the kitchen had been shorter
than usual, so he had a little more energy. Twenty
minutes after hanging up his apron he had the oxygen mask draped around his neck, was bundled
in his heaviest coat, and was working his way
down the stone ladder one level lower into the
caverns than he had ever been before. Seven levels down total. He had no idea how deep this
place went, but he'd have time to find out eventually. He had three more years on his shift before
heading back to Earth.

Down here it was colder than the higher levels
and he could see his breath. The air smelled dry
and stale, as if nothing had moved it in years.

Andy was used to that smell, and to the dusty, almost paperlike smell of the mummified corpses. But today, as he reached the seventh level, there was a new smell, faint yet distinct. The smell of antiseptic fought with the stale smell. It brought back memories of his mom taking him to the doctor when he was a kid back on Earth.

Andy flicked the beam of his light around on the floor, looking for any sign of disturbance. Nothing. It was clear that his boot prints were the only ones in the light dust. No one had been down here in longer than he wanted to think about.

He shook off the smell and memories of his childhood doctor and shone his light first down the dark tunnel to the right, then to the left. To the right, if he went far enough, he would approach the sealed-off sections of the alien hive. Andy, when given the choice, always went in the opposite direction, away from the alien hive. Robbing dead human bodies was one thing. Meeting an alien in a cold, dark tunnel was quite another.

Andy turned left and moved along, taking his time, not pushing himself too fast in order to conserve oxygen. Usually there was enough in the tunnels, but he had learned quickly the first time down here that taking an oxygen bottle along never hurt, especially on the long climb back up. And on the first trip down he'd learned about how cold it really was down here. Now he wore his thickest coat and gloves and the cold still got through.

Two corners and a short hike down a tunnel with an unusually low ceiling, he finally found a wide area with sleeping bunks carved into the stone wall on the left.

As the convicts had dug deeper and deeper into the rock, they carved new bunks closer to where they were working. As convicts fell ill, or died in accidents, or were shot by the guards, they were placed in the abandoned bunks and left to mummify in the extreme cold, dry air. This room had three bodies, one seemed fine, one had a missing arm, and a third had its head severed and placed on its chest. The head had a massive amount of damage to the bones where his nose and eyes used to be and the neck bones were crushed, not sawed or cut.

The day Andy found the first bodies he hadn't touched them and he hadn't slept a wink that night. But intrigued by a large gold ring on one of the bodies, after a week he had gone back, rationalizing that the convict sure didn't need that ring anymore. Now, after months of finding bodies, Andy had seen so many that this scene didn't even bother him.

He first checked the hands of all three bodies, finding only one silver wedding ring. Then he dug into the pockets and found only empty wallets and worn and faded family pictures. Then he checked the teeth, finding two silver caps in one and in the head that had been severed three gold fillings among the shattered teeth.

A fairly decent find. Whistling, he continued on down the tunnel, noticing now that the odor of antiseptic was getting stronger and stronger, even blocking out the intense cold. Chances are it was coming down a ventilation shaft from one of the Professor's labs.

Ahead, the tunnel turned sharply to the right, then back to the left, and Andy found himself facing an open heavy metal door, much newer than the original tunnel construction. Beyond the door the tunnel turned again sharply to the left and Andy could see a faint light.

"What the hell?" he said to himself, snapping off his own light. Slowly he moved through the door and onto the now smooth concrete floor of the tunnel. The floor in this area had been swept clean of dust and he was leaving gray footprints.

The smell of antiseptic now completely filled the air. Carefully, Andy stuck his head around the corner and looked into the bright lights of what appeared to be a lab of some sort just beyond another open airlock-style door. He could see white-tiled floors, shelves, and some lab equipment on a far wall, but not much else.

He waited a few breaths but no one moved, and no sound came from the lab, so he crept silently forward.

He'd heard a lot of strange rumors about the Professor and what went on behind the closed doors of this station, but he had made it a point not to pay attention. He figured it just wasn't his business.

But something open like this down here seemed just plain wrong, and he moved forward until he could see the contents on the shelves ahead of him.

Now, in robbing graves, he had seen a lot of human bodies, but it still took him a moment to register what he was seeing.

Shelf after shelf of human heads, all with wires and tubes leading from them into instrument panels, filled the room. The skin on most of the parts was a deep blue or black, and some had large patches of flaking. But yet they seemed full of fluid and somehow alive.

Andy moved slowly forward until he stood between five shelves of human heads on the right and three shelves of human heads on the left.

He stopped in front of one head with brown hair and looked at it closely. The hair was long and matted and the skin tone on this one seemed to be a pasty white. What looked to be an oxygen mask covered the nose and mouth and wires ran from about twenty different places on the side and forehead. The head was secured by a rubber ring around the neck that seemed to surge every few seconds. Obviously a liquid of some sort was being circulated through the head and brains.

"What the hell . . . ?" he said out loud.

His hand shaking, Andy slowly reached out and pulled the head up slightly by the hair.

The eyes opened.

Blue eyes.

The blue eyes of his old poker-playing buddy Charlie. Charlie, who had supposedly left for Earth unexpectedly, six months earlier.

Andy screamed and jumped backward square into the waiting arms of Larson. The man's grip on his shoulders felt like steel clamps and he fought in panicked kicks and twists to get free, to run away from those heads and those chilling blue eyes.

With one quick arm twist Larson took Andy to his knees in sharp pain.

Andy quit struggling. He just kept staring at the now sad blue eyes of his old friend, as if the head could understand what was happening, could recognize him, was somehow still thinking.

"Well," the Professor said, moving forward out of the shadows of the shelf of heads, most of whose eyes were now open and watching.

Green eyes. Blue eyes. Brown eyes. They all watched.

"It seems we have another volunteer for our program," the Professor said.

"Seems that way to me," Larson said, yanking Andy's hair back and making him look up at the Professor.

"What—what are you doing here?"

Kleist glanced around and then laughed. "I need these alive to keep the bodies in my labs alive. For some reason I can't fool the face-huggers without having the real head still hooked up." He gave Andy a good looking over. "He seems to be in good physical condition. Get him ready. His body just may be the one to carry our new queen. Now wouldn't that be a privilege, Andy?"

Andy screamed like a wildman and struggled to free himself, to force his way to his feet.

To run to the safety of the dark, cold tunnels and the dead convicts.

But he was no match for the cold, brute strength of Larson. With a quick blow to the back of the neck, Larson sent Andy into blackness.

Most of the heads on the shelves closed their eyes as if they had witnessed this sad sight before and didn't want to watch it again.

As indeed, many of them had.

The next time Andy opened his eyes, he looked down from the second shelf, the closest position to the door into the tunnels on the left.

He could still feel his body alive, somewhere

else. He could feel his heart pumping blood, his
arms floating, and something growing inside him.

The blackness of space and the faint light of a
thousand stars filled the bubble ceiling of the observation lounge. The room had been designed
and built by the Professor, stuck five hundred meters down a long stairway out on a rock outcrop-
ping so that it could be above the base. It had cost
a great deal extra, but the Professor and the de-
signers from the corporation thought it worth the
cost.

From almost every square foot of the lounge
the view of the rocky surface of Charon Base and
the stars was spectacular. The emptiness of the
rough surface of asteroid bathed in the faint light
from the sun and the even fainter light from the
sky full of stars.

But the lounge was very seldom used after the
first few months. It seemed that no one wanted a
reminder that they were living like rats in tunnels
under hundreds of meters of rock. And they didn't
want to think about how far they were from Earth
and the black sky full of stars reminded them of
that. Many felt that if they didn't think about it, it
didn't bother them.

Going to the observation lounge made them
think about it, made them realize they were
trapped.

So after six months of very little use Kleist
closed the bar that had filled one corner and just
left the lounge open to the few stragglers or the
occasional lovebirds. At one point the place had
been filled with plants, but even those were gone,

moved out or allowed to die off. Now only the empty containers remained, making the furniture and booths seem naked under the faint light. The overall feel was of a deserted living room or a forgotten old house.

Cray was the only occupant of the lounge as Joyce walked in and glanced around. She had guessed she would find him here. He seemed like the type to love the openness of the stars and she felt glad about being right. It pushed her forward with her plan.

He stood against the rail in front of the main window, staring off into the blackness.

"Is this a private moment of moody introspection," Joyce said as she moved up beside him, "or can anyone join?"

"By all means," Cray said. "Be my guest. Introspect all you want."

She smiled and glanced around at the empty room. "Seems we're the only ones who enjoy the view."

"That it does," Cray said without turning from the window. "Sort of reminds me of the old lover's leaps back home. See how the rocks slope off there." He pointed to where the edge of the cliff rounded off and disappeared into blackness below. "You have a place like that where you grew up?"

The memories of her and Danny parked in his old Ford at the top of Thunder Mountain flashed back through her mind. It would always take them an hour to get up there, but it was worth it. They used to sit in the dark, holding hands and staring at the stars. They used to talk night after night about how they would go into space when they got out of school, live in space, bring up a family among the stars.

On Thunder Mountain, on a blanket under the stars, she had lost her virginity.

She turned to Cray. "I sure did. How about you?"

He laughed. "Of course. And call me John."

"I'm Joyce."

He nodded, then turned back to face the stars. "We called our little hideaway Roman Way. It was a wide spot on the top of a small hill just outside of town. The hill looked out over the Kansas farmlands and was damn near the highest place in twenty miles."

"Roman Way? Like in roaming hands?"

Cray laughed and glanced at her. "Cute, but no. Actually a farmer named Barry Roman owned the land."

Joyce grinned. "Ours was called Thunder Mountain, named after a bad storm, I think."

He laughed softly and they both went back to watching the stars. After a moment Cray stirred and turned to her. "Tell me," he said. "What brings you out this far from the main Earth systems? Isn't that where most pilots ply their trade?"

Joyce reached into her back pocket and pulled out a small folding wallet. With a gentle flip she opened it and held it up in the faint light for Cray to see. "These are my reasons. Drake and Cass."

Cray studied the picture of her two kids, both dark-skinned like their mother. She watched him gaze at the picture, wishing she knew what he was thinking. Finally he said, "Good-looking kids."

"You got that right," she said. "At least as far as

I'm concerned. Of course, I'm their mother so I would think that."

Cray smiled. "Justified, in this case."

Joyce flipped the wallet closed and went back to looking at the stars. After a moment she decided to go on and tell him more, trust him a little more. "Their father was killed during the war and we barely made it. The kids live in Geneva now with my mother. I get fifty times the pay out here than I do in the central systems. That's why I took this haul one last time. After I'm back I can spend a few years with my kids. I sure do miss them."

"Sorry," Cray said softly. "I didn't mean to pry."

"No problem. It's just the way things are. You learn to live with it."

Joyce glanced around quickly, studying the ceiling and the walls around them. She needed his help, but she wasn't sure if she could trust him. Damn, this had been a dumb idea.

"Something wrong?" Cray asked after a moment.

"You seem like a straightforward-type guy."

"Thanks. I guess," he said, looking intently at her.

She took a deep breath. "You know, there are just some things in this world I don't think I *can* live with?"

Cray nodded, waiting.

Joyce flipped open her wallet again and pulled a slip of paper out from behind the picture of her children. She pulled it out just far enough for Cray to see. On it she had written, "Don't say anything. Please meet me on my ship in one hour."

Out loud she said, "This is a picture of my husband. Bugs killed him in the last days of the war.

For some reason I have problems living with that, and being this close to an entire hive of the things."

She slid the paper back behind the picture and put the wallet away.

"I can understand that," Cray said. "Some things really are hard to live with."

"Yeah," she said. "I'll be damn glad when I get headed for home."

They both turned to face the cold, black night and the thousand points of light so far away.

Joyce tried to keep her hands from shaking. She had just put her life into the hands of a total stranger. She didn't know why, but when it came right down to it she felt she could trust him. Besides, she had no one else to turn to and she needed his help.

Above her, just past her left shoulder, was Earth and her two children.

She kept her gaze away from that area of the black sky.

T-shirted Sergeant Green stormed through the main lab, his fists clenched in tight balls, his gray-eyed gaze focused intently ahead. His thick muscles rippled with power under the shirt and men and women in white coats scrambled out of his way like they would jump away from the path of a moving train. His movements just dared anyone to try to stop him, and no one did.

No one was stupid enough to even try.

He reached the Professor's outer private office on the far side of the lab and yanked the door open, almost pulling it off the hinges in the process.

Behind a large oak desk across what seemed like ten meters of thick white carpet sat Grace, the Professor's secretary. She glanced up as he wrenched the door open. She wore a tight maroon skirt and a white blouse open one button too far showing a little too much very real-looking skin.

The same basic thing she wore every day.

"Can I help you, Sergeant?" she said calmly, standing and moving into his path as he stormed toward her desk and started around it toward the Professor's inner office.

"I want to see Kleist right now!" He didn't even slow and started to brush right past her.

With what seemed to be a slight push, with very little force behind it, she knocked him into the oak wall sending an oil painting tumbling behind a couch.

The sergeant bounced off the wall, twisted off the couch, and instantly went into combat posture, crouched and facing her.

She stood upright, looking almost bored as she studied one of her nails. "I'm afraid he's in a meeting. He left strict instructions that he was not to be disturbed."

"Outta my way, bitch, or I swear I'll—"

"He was most insistent," she said, smiling at the sergeant. "Why don't I just make you an appointment and you can come back. I'm sure he has some time open tomorrow."

The sergeant's face turned bright red and he growled low in his throat. "I'll show you and that ass of a boss an *appointment*."

He again started for the door that led into the private back office.

Grace stepped lightly to the left and directly into his path, stopping him cold with one hand to his chest.

The sergeant raised his left hand to shove her aside, but she merely added, "Now, Sergeant, you wouldn't strike a woman, would you?"

"Yes," the sergeant said, but he had hesitated just long enough for Grace to get a firm hold on his forearm with her right hand and his T-shirt with her left. With a quick twisting motion she turned and flipped him over her shoulder and away from the Professor's door, into the middle of the huge white carpet.

"That's good, because I'm no woman," she said, laughing.

He landed square on his back with a loud thud and the sound of air forced from his chest. He twisted sideways and scrambled to his feet. Without a moment's hesitation he charged back at her like a bull at a red cape.

She hiked her skirt up slightly with one hand and caught him square across the side of the face with a high side kick.

This time the sergeant tumbled head over heels along the empty top of her desk and came up rolling, his hands on the desk chair Grace had been using.

"Really, Sergeant. Why can't you just make an appointment like everyone else? It would be so much simpler."

He again growled like an angry wolf. With a quick motion to the right, he faked her into a defensive stance, then hit her from the left with the chair. She staggered sideways, but didn't fall. Her fake skin wasn't even slightly cut where the chair had sliced across her face.

She ducked to the left to avoid his right hook, then kicked him again squarely in the face, her high heel digging a long, wide gash in his cheek.

The sergeant tumbled back onto the carpet and before he had time to move Grace kicked him twice more, once in the ribs, once more in the face.

He rolled hard over to get away from her, but she was inhumanly fast and was on him again with two more kicks to the head. "That'll teach you to stain the carpet." She kicked him again. "And that's for not making an appointment like a good little boy."

Through the haze of almost blackness he heard the Professor say, "That's enough, Grace. I'm sure the sergeant has learned his lesson."

Grace grabbed Green by the back of his shirt and like picking up a young child hauled him to his feet, turning him to face the Professor.

Kleist stepped closer and smiled. "I think I know what he's upset about."

The sergeant spit a mouthful of blood on the white carpet at the Professor's feet and then looked him directly in the eye. "You murdered one of my men, you bastard."

"As you witnessed, Sergeant, Private Choi deliberately destroyed an expensive specimen."

Green couldn't believe what he was hearing. "You killed him for that?"

"See my side of this, Sergeant," the Professor said. "Choi could easily have subdued the alien with a Taser, and yet chose not to. I call that a conscious act of sabotage."

"What? I should take you apart one ugly limb at a time."

Grace's grip on the back of the sergeant's shirt tightened and she lifted him slightly off the floor, holding one arm in a tight and very painful grip behind his back.

The Professor nodded to her that it was all right and she let him back down so his feet at least touched the floor. But she didn't ease the painful grip and he did his best to focus on the Professor and ignore the pain.

"As director of this facility, I felt obliged to authorize the maximum penalty."

"Choi was right," Green said, spitting another glob of blood on the white carpet. "You are insane."

The Professor laughed. "This is a scientific research establishment, not a military outpost. You're under my jurisdiction and will follow my orders."

The sergeant tried to make an unexpected lunge at the Professor but Grace held him firm, one hand on the back of his shirt, the other on his left arm in a lock grip.

The Professor only shook his head, then turned his back on the sergeant for a moment, seeming to think. When he turned back around he was frowning. "I'm tired of your men's insubordination and locker-room mentality. As of now Mr. Larson will relieve you of all duties. Grace will arrange for your and your men's immediate return to Earth. You and your grunts are an irritation I'm no longer prepared to endure."

The sergeant relaxed slightly in Grace's grip, not totally accepting what Kleist had said. He had come here expecting to die trying to kill the Professor, but somehow it had turned into freedom for him and his remaining men. That made no sense.

The Professor nodded to Grace. "Now, if you'll excuse me, I have business to attend to."

As Kleist's door closed with a soft click, Grace turned and shoved the sergeant forward through the office door into the lab. He stumbled forward, then fell, blood flowing down his face and the front of his shirt. He lay sprawled on the hard white tile of the main lab, staring up at Grace's unruffled short skirt, red hair, and slightly open white blouse.

"Get your men packing. I'll have a transport ready in two hours."

The sergeant struggled to his feet and stood weaving slightly, as if there were a slight breeze blowing him around. His mind was having trouble accepting what had just happened. Finally he nodded and turned to leave as everyone in the main lab silently watched.

"Oh, and, Sergeant," Grace said as she moved back into the office and to the desk.

He stopped and looked back at her. She picked up the desk chair and bent the metal leg back into shape with one hand before placing it on the carpet.

Then she looked up and smiled. "Next time make an appointment."

6

Captain Joyce Palmer
stood behind the pilot's chair of her ship *Caliban*
and let her hands glide over its cloth back. The familiar feel somehow gave her comfort and slowed
her breathing. She loved the slightly stale smell of
the ship's air mixed with the light odor of oil from
the control area. She felt in control when she was
in here.

She glanced around, automatically checking the
different boards, looking for warning lights like
she had done a hundred times in space. Now, here
in the hangar, most of the lights were showing
systems off or on standby. Nothing looked out of
the ordinary at all and that settled her jumping

nerves a little more. She always felt better when the machinery worked.

Would Danny have been mad at her for talking to Cray? Would Jerry? Would they both have said that she should keep to her own business and just leave this place. She knew that was exactly what they both would have said, yet she just couldn't let Jerry's death go. And she knew if Danny were still alive, he wouldn't let it go either.

She moved around and sat in her chair, letting her hands glide over the silent control panel, letting the feel of the familiar cushions hold her. She wouldn't be able to live with herself if she didn't try to stop this madman. There was a plague running wild on this station and it was killing people. It had killed one of her oldest friends. It was a virus of terror and sudden death, one man's madness killing hundreds.

Maybe she could stop it, or maybe she would die trying. Either way, she couldn't go on living without doing something.

Behind her she heard the sound of someone entering, walking up the long ramp from the deck. She tensed and waited, half expecting the Professor or Larson and some of his goons, but after a moment Cray stuck his head in. She let out a silent breath and motioned for him to come forward and take the chair beside her.

"I'm not sure this is wise," he said as he slid into Deegan's usual seat.

"Neither am I," she said. "There's a problem here and it has become very personal for me. You're about my only choice to turn to for help."

Cray shrugged.

Here goes, Joyce said to herself. No turning

back now. She reached under her seat and pulled out a miniature video disk. She held it up for Cray to see. "This was slipped to me yesterday."

Again Cray said nothing, so Joyce went on. "Professor Kleist is Z.C.T. Corporation's golden boy, right? Intense, but he gets results."

She slipped the disk into a small slot in her control panel and pointed to the large monitor. "This is how he does it. I hope you have a strong stomach."

The monitor flickered slightly before the picture focused on the tanks that filled the walls in the Professor's lab. Row after row of bodies floated in liquid, tubes running into panels in front of each. White-coated technicians worked in front of the wall at control panels and computer monitors. It was obvious from how the picture was being taken that it was from a hidden camera, most likely tucked into the pocket of a lab coat with only the lens peeking out.

Joyce noticed that Cray wasn't that startled by what he saw, but he did push himself back away from the monitor deeper into his chair.

The picture focused on one body, zooming in until only the head and chest area were visible. The skull was hairless and the face totally covered by a face-hugger, or what looked to be one. The chest of the body seemed to be moving, pulsing like it had a heart ten times too big that was pounding out of control.

Cray watched the screen while Joyce watched him.

The movement inside the chest went on for only a few more seconds, then suddenly the skin ripped in a quick spider pattern, like a rock hitting a large glass window. A small alien exploded from the chest in a spurt of black blood and frantic squirming, swimming off into the liquid and disappearing along the bottom of the tank.

The force of the eruption sent the body twisting in the tank, yanked back and forth by the lifelines connecting it to the machines.

Then the monitor flickered and went blank.

Cray took a deep breath, then slowly turned to Joyce. "All right, what's the problem? An experimental alien birth from a cloned body. Not pleasant to watch, but not a crime that I know of."

Joyce snorted. So that was the Professor's line. Cloned bodies? No wonder so many people were letting him get away with this. Most of them just didn't know, or didn't have enough courage to question his explanation.

She reached forward and punched a few keys on her board, and the monitor lit up again at the start of the disk. She jumped it quickly to the point where the alien was ripping a hole in the chest of its host, then froze the picture.

"See that?" She pointed to a small mark on one arm of the body, the arm that had been turned away from the glass wall and the room and only twisted into camera view because of the force of the alien birth.

Cray leaned forward. "What is it?"

"Just a second and I'll show you."

Joyce's fingers flew over the keys in front of her, and the still picture on the monitor zoomed in closer and closer on the mark until it became clear exactly what it was.

"A tattoo?" Cray said, leaning forward and

studying the mark. "A tattoo of a black raven? On a clone? That would make no sense at all."

"That's because that body isn't a clone. I doubt if any of them in that tank are." Joyce pulled a cigarette out of her vest pocket and lit it, half surprised that her hands weren't shaking much more than they were. "The Professor has come up with some pretty amazing stuff, but I doubt this level of human cloning is one of them."

She lit her cigarette and let the smoke soothe her as Cray stared at the monitor. Finally she said, "The person you see there was named Jerry. My husband Danny and I were with him when he got that tattoo done in Melbourne twelve years ago."

Joyce pushed the sleeve of her vest up until it rode over her shoulder and then turned for Cray to see the small black raven there. "We were such close friends we thought it would be great to have the same tattoo. The Black Raven was the name of a bar we used to meet at while in college."

Cray glanced at her tattoo, then back at the screen. Then he seemed to sink into the copilot's chair like a heavy weight was pushing him down.

Joyce rolled down her sleeve and took a long pull on her cigarette. "Jerry supposedly died last month. Faulty airlock is what they said. Explosive decompression is what the official report and what his death certificate says. I know. I checked."

She pointed at the monitor with the frozen close-up of Jerry's black raven. "They should've had to scrape him off the walls of that airlock but, surprise, there he is. Or at least what's left of him."

Joyce dropped back into her pilot's chair and

tapped the control panel. The picture on the monitor disappeared and in another moment the miniature video disk popped out. She took it, glanced at Cray, and then returned the disk to the hiding place under her seat.

Then she swung around to face him. "Well, there's not much doubt the Professor has lost it. The question is what are you going to do about it. No, what are *we* going to do about it?"

Cray shook his head without turning to face Joyce. "You don't know what you're asking."

"I know this," Joyce said. "Kleist's a psycho who's killing people for his own gain. He's got to be stopped. You have to let Z.C.T. know what's going on out here. Someone back there must have an ounce of sanity left."

Cray shook his head slowly from side to side. "It's not that easy."

Joyce grabbed the arm of Cray's chair and swung it around until he was facing her. She leaned forward and grabbed him by the shirt collar, pulling him toward her sharply. "I want to live to see my kids again, you chicken-shit piece of a man. I'm risking everything even talking to you."

"I know," Cray said softly. "I understand better than you would imagine. But there's much more that you should know, especially about me."

She let go of his collar and he dropped back into the chair. She took a long pull off her cigarette. "I'm listening."

Cray took a deep breath and sat up. "You trusted me, I suppose I now need to trust you."

Outside the ship the sound of footsteps running up the gangway echoed through the control room. "What the hell?" Joyce shouted and sprang to her feet to meet three of the Professor's men all carrying Kramers, fully cocked and set on automatic.

"Nobody move!" Larson shouted. He was the fourth man through the door. "Keep your mouths shut and your hands where I can see them."

The three guards swarmed around Joyce and Cray.

Joyce turned to Cray. "You bastard! I should have known."

"You deaf, bitch?" one of the guards said, and hit Joyce across the side of the head with the butt of his rifle. The pain took her legs out from under her and she rolled back against her pilot's chair. Through pain-watered eyes she saw Cray move.

Almost without effort he grabbed the guard who had hit her by the neck and twisted. The sound of the guard's neck snapping filled the small control room like a gunshot.

A second guard fired a blast from the rifle, but Cray had twisted the body of the now-dead guard in his arms around to take the force of the blow. Blood splattered against the wall as a few stray rounds ricocheted inside the ship.

Now the smell of charred flesh choked the air as Joyce fought to clear her head.

Almost effortlessly, Cray tossed the dead body at one guard while taking the other down with a quick kick to the head. With what seemed like a lightning-fast movement to Joyce's slowed-down senses, he was on his knees scooping up the dead guard's rifle when Larson said, "Go ahead. Pick it up."

Cray froze, the gun just barely touching his fingers, as Larson smiled at him. Larson held a forty-five pistol pointing directly at Cray's head.

The remaining two live guards quickly regained their feet and yanked Cray into a standing position, quickly binding his arms behind his back.

Joyce fought to get to her feet, to help Cray, but as she did one guard kicked her solidly in the side of the head and the pain took her into blackness. Her last thought was a simple one.

She had been right about Cray after all. Too bad she wasn't going to get a chance to tell him.

Hank ambled into the main lounge, doing his best to look calm and unhurried as he wound his way through the plants and tables to the bar. Actually, he was in more of a panic than he had been in in years. Joyce had stood him up for dinner last night and hadn't returned to her room at all. This morning, while looking for her, he had discovered from Jonathan that she had a copy of the video of Jerry's body in the tank. He was hoping he would have been the one to tell her about Jerry's death, but now he couldn't even find her. And as the day wore on he became more and more worried.

He ambled up to the bar and dropped onto a stool. "Vodka tonic?" Jonathan asked as he slipped a napkin in front of Hank. "Looks like you need it."

Hank nodded and Jonathan moved back to the well. The words "looks like you need it" were a code and meant that Jonathan had news he would be passing with the drink. Hank kept himself relaxed and looked wearily at the other people scattered around the lounge until Jonathan returned with the drink.

The underground movement against the Professor had discovered that the bar was a fairly safe place to pass notes and because of all the constant cleaning the staff did, they had every hidden camera and microphone spotted. They knew the exact dead spots in the room.

Jonathan sat the drink down on the napkin and Hank immediately picked it up, feeling the piece of paper attached to the wet outside of the glass.

He swung the stool around so that his back was turned at about a forty-five-degree angle from the bar and toward the main entrance. Then he pretended to drink, reading the note through the clear liquid and the glass.

"Professor has Joyce and Cray. Both still alive. Meeting at seven at #8 to plan."

Hank's stomach twisted and he glanced at the small note one last time before swinging back more directly to face the bar, keeping the note covered with his hand. His worst fears had been confirmed. Joyce was in the Professor's hands, and if they didn't do something quickly her body would soon be floating in that tank. Or worse, she would be put out in the alien section to serve as breeding stock for the Professor's pets.

He glanced at where Jonathan stood, casually cleaning the bar. He didn't look very happy either. He was probably feeling responsible for her capture and he would be there tonight also. Maybe it was finally time to move against the Professor and his men. Maybe they had waited long enough.

Hank downed the last of the drink and placed the glass on the bar, but he didn't let go of it. Jonathan saw the movement and moved unhurriedly back to him. "Need another?"

"Nope, thanks. One's enough. I've got a long night ahead of me."

Jonathan nodded and picked up the glass with the note still stuck to it a fraction of a second after Hank had released it. "I hear you there," he said. In a few seconds the note, along with the ice and lime in the drink, would be ground up in the garbage disposal.

"See ya," Hank said and slipped off the stool.

From the exchange Hank knew that Jonathan was thinking the same thing he was. Maybe it was time they finally quit sulking around and started moving. Maybe if they were all lucky the Professor and Larson would both be dead before the night was out. And Joyce would be back in his arms.

That would make it a great night.

But that assumed that Joyce would live. The Professor's victims didn't have a habit of living very long at all.

He forced that thought out of his mind and went in search of his Marine contact, a young private named Choi.

At that moment Hank had no idea just how late he really was.

Sergeant Green glanced down at his men as they buckled into their flight harnesses in the "cattle" compartment of the transport. It was a bullet-shaped room with two benches on either side. Vertical bar handles were attached to the walls between the seats, and seat belts and shoulder harnesses hung off the walls. Green glanced down the line at his men, all joking and happy.

Still, what seemed like an enormous number of empty seats near the tail haunted Green. Nineteen men were going home out of his original forty. Those were huge, unacceptable losses, especially on an assignment as stupid as this one. There would be an investigation when they reached Earth of the Professor and his little operation. Sergeant Green would make sure of that.

"Man, can you believe this?" Private Young said from down the row. "We're actually going to see the back end of this damn place."

"Yeah, imagine that," Private Richerson said. "What's the plan, Sarge?"

Green took a deep breath and tried to shake the feeling that something was wrong. They were going home. What could be wrong with that? "We're to rendezvous with the battle cruiser *Saundakaur*, then deep-freeze it from there."

Young shivered. "I hate those ice boxes."

"Price you pay," Richerson said, "for working out in the butt end of the universe."

Grace's voice echoed over the intercom system. "Buckle in tight, boys. We're on our way."

Green glanced up at the speaker, startled that she was on board. He'd love another shot at her, only this time on his terms and under his conditions. Then he'd see how well that pile of bolts and tubes in a skirt would do. Maybe before this trip was over he'd get that chance.

"Wow, the voice of God," Richerson said.

"More like his secretary," Green muttered as the roar of the engines started and the acceleration pushed them all into their harnesses.

But instead of the steady, six-minute burn needed to clear Charon's gravity well, the engines quickly throttled back and Green could feel the ship banking in a hard, tight turn.

"Whoa!" Young said and others cursed the change.

"What gives, Sarge?" someone shouted.

"Damned if I know," Green said, "but I got a bad feeling about this." He cussed himself for being so stupid. No way was the Professor going to let them go. He couldn't afford to let him—or anyone else for that matter—make it back to Earth alive. He was going to crash the ship back into the planet and call them dead by accident. Case closed.

Sergeant Green unsnapped his harness, grabbed his pistol, and started toward the front, shouting orders to the man at the very head of the line. "Lynch, get that door to the cockpit open. The rest of you stay belted in and brace yourselves. This might get bumpy."

Lynch had his harness undone and was at the door as Green joined him. "It's locked!" he shouted over the roar of the thrusters.

"Override it!" Green shouted back and together they fought to open the door.

What seemed like hours went by, but Green knew it was only seconds as Lynch worked expertly on the lock, his fingers flying over and around it. Finally, with a hard yank, he shoved the door open and Green was through into the cockpit of the shuttle with his gun cocked and ready.

Two empty pilot seats greeted him.

"Shit! We're on remote." Green stood braced against the back of the pilot's seat, watching as the shuttle turned and braked into an old shuttle docking area. From the look of the instruments and where they were headed, it seemed Kleist didn't plan on killing them by crashing the shuttle. That way he could save the ship and maybe reuse it down the road. But if not a crash, what the hell was he doing?

Sergeant Green scanned the docking area ahead looking for any sign of life. But there was nothing. The place looked as if it had been unused for years.

"Sir," Lynch said from where he was braced on the other side of the cockpit. "Isn't that the . . ."

"Shit!" Green said, the sudden realization of where they were heading hitting him. He turned to his men. "Get suited up, full armor. Fast. That son of a bitch is dropping us right into the middle of the alien sector."

Eighteen harnesses unsnapped simultaneously and nineteen men and their sergeant went quickly to work, struggling against the forces of the landing shuttle to don full battle armor and get weapons out of storage in the crowded "cattle" area of the small transport.

By the time the landing thrusters finally cut off thirty seconds later and the shuttle moved automatically toward the airlock door, Sergeant Green and his men were ready.

Green looked back at his men and made a decision. They were now in a war. It was them against the Professor, with an alien hive in the middle. He had underestimated the Professor before. He wouldn't do it again. It was now his job to take the son of a bitch down. And take him down hard.

"Check your ammunition!" Green shouted as everyone shouldered arms.

"Shit!" Lynch said from beside him. A few other

curses came from down the line. "Blanks, sir. Everything's been switched. Nothing but blanks. We're screwed."

"Hold it down!" Green shouted, and his men immediately quieted. Outside the airlock clanked into place and the opening and sealing process began. That side door was going to open and stay open into the alien sector in just a few seconds. If they were lucky none of the bugs would be waiting outside. But it wouldn't take them long to arrive.

"Unload the useless stuff from the guns and shoulder your weapons. Keep your ammunition belts on and full of the blanks. I want a tight formation following me the moment that door cracks open. Stragglers get left behind. Understood?"

Everyone nodded and the useless ammunition clattered on the deck of the shuttle like a hailstorm on a tin roof.

"Full armor. Helmets down and locked, but no talking on the intercom system. Hand signals only, no exceptions. Understood?"

Again as a unit everyone nodded and helmets clicked into place and were locked. He didn't have time to explain to them that the Professor was probably watching them at this very moment and that he probably had their helmet intercoms wired. If he could get to all their ammunition, he could easily do that, too. But Green doubted if Kleist had cameras and speakers on all areas of the alien sector. That was a fact Green was going to count on to save his men's lives.

"Get ready," Green said as he moved to the closest spot near the airlock and stood waiting for whatever would be on the other side. "And keep the noise down. We go silent."

Nineteen men crowded in behind him, moving almost as a unit.

The airlock door slid open.

The smell of rotten eggs hit first, followed by a blast of hot, humid air.

Nothing moved in the slime-filled shadows.

Green took a quick look to the left, then ducked out of the ship and in a crouch moved silently but quickly down the corridor to the right away from the ship and the docking area.

Like a silent snake, his men followed in close formation.

Followed him unarmed into the heart of an alien hive.

There was silence in Professor Kleist's office as the last of Green's men disappeared off the only monitor near that entrance to the alien sector. Finally the Professor swung around in his chair and addressed Larson, who stood behind him.

"Any chance we can see what they're doing in there?"

Larson shook his head. "Not until they get near this side of the alien sector, and they'll never make it that far."

"Don't be so sure," the Professor said.

Larson smiled and reached over Kleist's desk and punched up the center screen. On it was a map of the alien sector. Twenty points of light grouped tightly together near the farthest entrance moved slowly down one passageway. "I did manage to put tracers in their com links. We'll see right where each of them dies."

"Good," the Professor said, his head nodding, his hands steepled in front of him. "Nice work? Now if you could just guarantee that none of them make it back here."

Larson nervously glanced at the monitor and then back at the Professor. "I think I can, sir. They're unarmed, twenty klicks deep in an alien hive. No one, not even the Marines, could live through that."

Kleist nodded. "I tend to agree with you, but just to be sure, let's post double guards on all airlocks between the human and alien sectors. If one or two of them do manage to sneak through, I want them turned back."

He laughed. "Besides, we couldn't let the queen be deprived of such good breeding material, now could we?"

7

The nightmare continued.

The blackness of the moonless night covered the old green Ford like a smothering blanket that nothing could crawl out from under. John Cray had been given the used car by his father for a wedding present just six months earlier. He'd had it repainted and some much-needed body work done first. But now, as the starter ground on and on, he wished he'd worked on the engine first. A stalled motor, probably nothing more than a loose switch or wire, had them four short kilometers from the spaceport, sitting in the most dangerous of dark nights.

Four impossible miles with the aliens swarming closer to this area every hour.

"Damn it!" He pounded on the wheel. "Start, damn you." He fought the ignition one more time, but it was clear from the grinding sound that there would be no more distance from this car tonight, or maybe ever. He knew that much about cars.

And about aliens.

"John," Linda said softly and touched his arm.

Her soft touch calmed him somewhat and he stopped. Angrily he twisted the key to off and turned to face his beautiful bride in the faint light from the dashboard.

He could see the worry on her face. Her long blond hair was pulled back tight making her face like a small, white moon in the faint light. Her clean soap smell filled the car like a fine perfume. All he wanted to do was hold her, curl up in a warm bed, tell her they would be fine.

But they wouldn't be fine until somehow they reached the spaceport and joined the evacuation off Earth. In this area of the planet that was their only hope and they both knew it.

He reached out and patted the soft skin of her leg, doing his best to fight down his panic and reassure her, as well as himself. "If we stay here and keep quiet we should be all right until someone comes along."

She nodded. She had trusted him since the first night they had met at the Christmas party. She worked as an account executive for the Grant Corporation, the same corporation he did troubleshooting work for on computers. The same company he spied for after this night.

"If there's no traffic tonight, we'll walk at first light. We should be able to make it to the port in a few hours. The corporation will have enough ships to get us to Earth orbit."

She was about to say something when, as he watched in shocked terror, an alien appeared out of the dark shadows directly behind her.

It was a huge creature with a black bony shell and thousands of teeth in saliva-filled jaws.

Before he even had time to scream a warning it smashed the window behind Linda and with a four-fingered hand around her chest yanked her back against the door.

"No!" He frantically reached for her, straining against the seat belt he still wore.

"John!" she screamed. Her eyes were wide with terror and disbelief. "John!" She fought at the hand on her chest fighting to pull the slick black fingers off her.

Behind her the alien hissed deep and long.

Another alien hand snaked in the window on the other side of her, and the awful smell of sulfur and rotten eggs filled the car like a choking gas.

He grabbed for her, but the seat belt still held him and all he could touch across the car was her leg. He grabbed it and tried to pull her away from the bug as she fought madly to pry the hands away from her.

Then, with a sudden hard yank from the alien, she was bent over double, her skin pulled roughly from his grasp. Her seat belt snapped, and with her head between her legs, she was pulled roughly through the window. Her legs and back left bloody strips of skin and cloth on the broken glass.

"No!" he screamed again, fighting to free himself from the safety belt. But it seemed snagged on something, or he wasn't pushing the right area of the clasp or something. It wouldn't release. He fought at it, ripping at it, struggling to free himself so he could save his wife.

But the nightmare continued.

The belt wouldn't let him go.

Linda's screams were cut off in the dark night beyond the car as he fought with that buckle, twisting at the straps, struggling to be free.

The nightmare continued.

"He's coming around," a voice said through the thick blackness and the terror.

The horror retreated slightly, only to be replaced by the memory of Charon Base and another nightmare. A nightmare of a mission gone bad.

"Good," another voice said from his other side. "Did you get anything?"

"Nothing of any worth."

John Cray struggled back to the reality, the sounds of Linda's screams still echoing in his mind.

He was totally nude with large straps holding his arms and his legs like firm, rough hands. Another strap held his forehead tight against the back of a huge padded chair. Tubes ran from both his arms, the area above his heart, and the sides of both legs to nearby machines. His penis and balls were encased in what looked to be a large suction hose that extended under his ass. Three needle inserts had been stuck into his brain and a mass of wires ran from them to something he couldn't see behind him.

"He still denies everything," Larson said, "and he is somehow blocking the mind probes."

Cray opened his eyes, letting the image of Linda go for the moment.

In front of him stood Professor Kleist in a white smock. He looked huge, like a white judge standing at the pearly gates as Linda's screams faded totally away in the back of his mind.

The Professor smiled when he noticed that Cray's eyes were open. He knelt down so he could look at his captive directly. "Why are you doing this?"

Cray just blinked, not responding. He tried to think of the good times with Linda, but they just wouldn't come. Only being trapped by that seat belt in the middle of that awful night. It was the only thought of her that he had at the moment.

"We know you're *not* really working for Z.C.T., but for Grant Corporation, so you can stop pretending. Just tell us what you know and you'll die painlessly. I can promise you that."

Cray thought of how he had finally freed himself from the seat belt during that awful night. It had been too dark to follow Linda and the alien's tracks, but he had still tried, over and over, scrambling through the brush and trees, calling her name, begging for her to be all right. But he never saw her again, and her body was never found.

He had been sitting in the middle of the road shouting and crying when the Marine transport had picked him up.

The Professor glanced up over Cray's shoulder at Larson, then, disgusted, he turned back to Cray. "Continue to try my patience and you'll suffer beyond all imagining."

Cray focused on the Professor. "I ... I don't know ... don't know what you want."

The Professor leaned back and half smiled. "Then I will tell you exactly what we know and what we want." He again glanced over Cray's shoulder and then back at Cray. "I will grant you," he said, "that your plan was an audacious one. I admire that, to be honest with you, especially the holo of my old friend at headquarters. I'm amazed that he could keep a straight face when he was doing that for you. I even bet you were sitting in his office watching him record it, weren't you?"

Kleist smiled as Clay fought to keep the memory of that day in the Z.C.T. headquarters from his mind. But from the look on the Professor's face, he hadn't succeeded.

"You were hoping," the Professor said, after glancing again over Cray's shoulder, "to make me so paranoid about infiltration that I'd hand you the Chimera Project data without a second thought."

The Professor laughed hard and sharp and then moved closer to Cray so he was looking him directly in the eye. Cray noticed the Professor's breath smelled dirty and sour, as if his insides were rotting out. He could only wish.

"You made one fatal mistake a long time ago," the Professor said, grinning right in Cray's face, gloating with brown teeth just inches from Cray's face. "Z.C.T. agents above grade nine have a security code surface-coated on their right kidney. You, a supposed grade twelve, did not. That was clear when we checked you in decontamination when you first walked onto the station."

Cray struggled to think of his wife, of the night she died, anything but the implications of what the Professor had said.

Kleist leaned back and laughed for what seemed to be much too long. Finally he caught his breath and faced Cray straight on again. "That's right. We've known you worked for the Grant Corporation all along. For years now. We let you feed us the Taser and gel data to get our trust. Wasn't that nice of us?"

Again he laughed, but this time he cut it off quickly. "We wanted to know what you were after, who your contacts were. We've netted quite a haul thanks to you. Including Captain Palmer."

Cray fought against the belts to sit upright. "No, no. She's not . . ."

The Professor laughed. "I may be as mad as they all say I am, but I'm not stupid." He nodded to Larson who moved around into Cray's line of sight. He was carrying a square box with instruments attached to one side.

"We even came up with a plan to get you out here, away from any support you might have in the corporation. We even made it seem as if it was your idea. We needed you here so you'd tell us everything you know. And trust me, you will tell us."

The Professor glanced at Larson and nodded. Then he stared directly into Cray's eyes. "Otherwise, you'll soon discover there is such a thing as a fate worse than death."

Larson turned the box and held it inches from Cray's face so that Cray could look directly into the small window. Then he turned the box so Cray could look directly into the slime-covered underside of an alien face-hugger.

He turned the box so that Cray could see his own living death.

"No!" Cray screamed as the box got closer.

He fought against the belts on the chair, fought against the seat belt as Linda was hauled through the window of the car.

Fought against the thought of that thing on his face.

He lost all three fights.

And the nightmare continued.

8

At the second corridor after leaving the airlock, Green had his men pull the metal grate off a large ventilation duct, then led them inside, shutting the grate behind them. The ducts in this area were carved out of solid stone like separate tunnels. Shoulder width and just barely tall enough for them to run in slightly stooped over, Green figured the ventilation tunnels were their best hope for the moment. They would have no chance at all in the main tunnels.

In this area of the hive there were very few signs of alien habitation, and in this ventilation tunnel there wasn't even any of the alien slime. That was a good sign, at least for the time being.

He had no doubt that the aliens had penetrated

the ventilation system, but there would be fewer of them. Plus he hoped the men could move more quietly through the ventilation system, staying away from any of the main chambers and as far away as possible from the queen. And if there was a fight, he would lose fewer men in a close quarter drill than in an open and high-ceilinged corridor.

After three hundred meters the shaft suddenly widened into a small room with a grate leading back into the main halls, another shaft leading off in the direction they were going, and a shaft crossing vertically, dropping into blackness.

Robinsen went into the room first, his light checking the corners and both up and down, then he signaled to the sergeant all-clear.

Green entered the area and went to the vertical shaft. It dropped farther than the beam from his light would shine. Handholds were cut into the side of the rock going both up and down and Green studied them for a moment before nodding. They would work. Not as good as the ladders in the main corridors, but these would serve.

Green pointed down and motioned for O'Keefe behind him to join Robinsen on the point.

Green knew their only hope was down. He'd studied all the plans for the base, as well as the rough tunnel layouts left behind after the last of the prisoners were taken off. He knew there were vast levels of tunnels under both the human base and the alien sector, all sealed off. If somehow he could get his men into them they might be able to work their way back to the human section and pay the Professor a surprise visit.

While they waited for Robinsen and O'Keefe to

signal the all-clear for the next level, Green had Lynch take apart one of their com units. It would be nice if they could use them, but until they were checked out he wasn't going to chance letting the Professor know where they were or what they were planning.

And that, for the moment, they were still alive.

Lynch made fast work of the helmet and within a few seconds was pointing to a tiny black dot attached to the underside of the mouth guard. "Tracer bug," he whispered. "There may be more."

Green nodded just as Robinsen signaled the all-clear.

He pointed to four of his men and indicated they should take off their headsets and all body armor and leave them. All nodded and did what they were told, letting the armor lay like the discarded white skins of dead humans.

Three levels down he had seven more men take off their helmets, com links, and body armor and put them in a cross corridor outside a ventilation grate. He'd let Kleist think they were putting up a running fight, losing a few men at a time.

The next level six more of the men did the same.

At the lowest level of the alien hive he had the last com links and helmets left beside a grate going into a main hall, including his own. Now all twenty of them were only wearing their brown pants and combat boots, brown T-shirts, and ammunition belts strapped over their shoulders.

Green had everyone stop and look for any more tracer bugs on any of the equipment and on their clothes. Like monkeys picking lice, they split up into pairs and inspected each other carefully, but quickly. Green checked Lynch while Lynch checked him.

Everyone came up negative. It seemed all the bugs were on the armor. Good. Now if the Professor just bought his decoys.

They had been running very silent and so far had been lucky not to be found by an alien. But if his memory served him correctly, on the next level down they were going to have to make some noise to get through a blockage. Enough noise to attract every damn alien in the place.

Robinsen signaled the all-clear to the next level and one by one nineteen Marines went down the narrow shaft.

In this small intersection the ventilation tunnel going on down had been sealed shut with what looked to be part of the wall carved to fit the hole exactly and then cemented into place. The plug on the hole could only be a meter thick, or it might be as wide as five meters.

A thin layer of dust covered everything and the air smelled stale in the small intersection. They had been so long in the rotten egg smell of the alien hive that it wasn't until one of the men coughed softly from the dust that Green even noticed the alien smell's absence. They must be a long ways from the main dens and the queen. Maybe they'd get lucky, but he discounted that thought quickly.

Green posted guards above and down both side tunnels, and told the men to conserve on the lights. Then he had Lynch and Robinsen gather around him.

"Seems we're a distance from the hive here," he whispered. "But we need to keep going down." He pointed at the sealed-off area. "Since we have no ammunition or explosives that I know of, anyone have any ideas how we can get down there quietly. Or if not quietly, quickly? And then seal it behind us?"

"My ex-wife's cooking would eat through that in a second," Lynch whispered and shrugged. Robinsen punched him lightly and Green smiled.

"Since, unfortunately, she's not with us," he whispered, "you two check with the others to see if they have any ideas."

Both nodded and silently moved away. With his men scattered around him Green went to the center of the small room and sat on the rock plug. He knew the longer they stayed in one place the more likely an alien would track them.

But ten meters down through a solid rock plug was their best hope at long-term survival. It was worth a little time to find a way.

While faint whispering from his men went on around him he closed his eyes and did his best to bring back up the vision of the rough prisoner maps he had looked at two years earlier. If they did get through, they were going to need his memory to keep them from getting lost in the maze of rock tunnels below.

"The Marines are gone," Hank said to the five men gathered around him in the circle of bright lamplight. The glow outlined the old tunnel carved out of rock six levels below the human section. The tunnel at this point was as high as his dad's old barn roof and about as wide. The air was dry, thin, and biting cold. Hank could see his breath in the lamplight and a fog seemed to form in the center of their group as they talked.

Bunk beds were carved in the rock wall opposite of where they gathered and one mummified prisoner's body lay curled on a top one, his back to the meeting. From where Hank stood the body looked peaceful and he envied it for that.

Their footsteps in the dust were the only sign anyone had been down in this tunnel for years and years. The six of them had had three meetings before like this one, all in different sections of the old tunnels.

"Gone?" Jonathan, the bartender, asked. "How? When?"

"I went to find Private Choi, my contact, and their bunk room was cleaned out. The guy cleaning the floors there said they had been shipped home."

"They're not totally gone," Ray said softly. Ray was a quiet guy with dark hair and more doctorate degrees than the rest of them combined. He had been the one who had gotten the secret film on Jerry's body. He worked with and around the Professor a great deal, as well as having access to the computers at times.

Ray glanced around at the group in the lamplight and then went on. "The Professor promised them a flight home, then dumped them on the far side of the alien sector. They were alive when they landed, that much I do know. But I doubt if they'll make it back here."

"Shit," Jonathan said. "You got any proof of that on tape?"

"Wish I did," Ray said, shaking his head sadly. The silence in the tunnel seemed to grow louder, pressing in against the thin wall the light had put up around them, making the circle of safety seem ever smaller. Six men stood inside that circle, lost in what the news of the Marines being gone meant.

Hank stared at the body of the prisoner in the shadows on the far wall. Gray coveralls hung over the body with a layer of white dust making his upper side look almost sun-bleached. It seemed so peaceful, yet Hank knew he hadn't died in peace. Hank doubted the Marines would die easy either. If he knew them, and Sergeant Green, they wouldn't go down without a fight.

Hank kept staring at the mummified body, thinking about what it meant to wipe out an entire company of Marines. The Professor had done it almost without a fight in less than three years, and would probably get away with it. How could the six of them and a few other loyal friends now stop such a madman? It didn't seem possible.

And maybe it wasn't, but the least they could do was try to save Joyce. Hank turned to Ray. "You know where they're keeping Captain Palmer?"

Ray nodded. "Cell Block Sixteen. I don't have a clue how she is, though."

"Is there a ventilation duct near there?"

Kent, who worked in maintenance, knelt and unrolled a bunch of large maps on the dusty floor. He thumbed through about ten before pulling one to the top and holding it flat. "Here and here," he said after a moment of study, pointing to marks on the maps. "In the halls outside the cells. They're not secured as far as I know."

"And we can get there from here?"

Kent nodded. "Sure can. Hell, you can get damn near anywhere in this base from these old tunnels and ventilation shafts that run through the base walls. What do you have in mind?"

Hank knelt and indicated that the others join him closer to the maps. "I think it's time we started a revolution," he said, studying the floor plan where Kent had pointed and at the square labeled CELL BLOCK SIXTEEN. "And since we're outnumbered, I think Captain Joyce Palmer would be a great addition to this side of the fight."

Hank looked around at his five friends. All were nodding. It seemed the loss of the Marines had got to them all. This time there was no arguing about waiting, no thought of just sitting and hoping the Professor would screw up somehow. Now they were ready to act.

And since he seemed to have a plan, they were ready to follow him.

"Here's my idea," Hank said.

Five men leaned in closer as Hank's frosty breath misted the air above the maps.

The Professor stood in front of a huge, reinforced window staring into the blackness of a very special cage. Somewhere in that blackness was his success, an alien like no other alien.

His baby.

A human body with its arms, legs, and head cut off and a gaping hole in its chest where a young alien had once emerged had been tossed in on the floor as food for his creation. He knew the creature was in there, back in the shadows, waiting. The Professor knew without a doubt how huge it was. He knew it was as big as any queen, because he had watched it grow.

But now, finally, it had reached maturity. Now he would finally know just how much his success meant.

The sound of the door opening behind him broke his thoughts and he turned to nod to Larson before returning his attention to the blackness beyond the glass.

When Larson halted behind him, the Professor spoke without turning. "Did our guest have anything further of interest to offer?"

"No. I'm pretty sure we've got everything. The prospect of a kiss from that face-hugger loosened his tongue real well, you might say."

The Professor gave Larson a sharp glance. "Spare me your pathetic attempts at humor."

There was a moment of silence as the Professor continued to stare into the blackness.

Finally Larson spoke again. "The pilot, Captain Palmer? She's clean. Cray's mission was apparently solo. Palmer just got in the way because of the death of her friend, Jerry."

"Jerry?"

"A tech guy we used up about two months ago. No one special."

Kleist nodded. "And the copy of the film she had?"

"Still working on where that came from. Might have been one of the techs or maybe a doctor. I'll find him."

"Or her," the Professor said. "Don't overlook the women. As for Captain Palmer, she's more trouble now than she's worth. Give her to the aliens. The livestock could use some boosting. That will be all."

After a moment Kleist heard the door close behind him and he was once again alone with his creation.

"Come to Papa," he said into the blackness as he pressed against the glass. "I've got some nice meat for you. Aren't you hungry?"

But for the moment nothing moved in the blackness beyond the glass.

9

The memory of the first day her kids went snow skiing had been keeping Joyce contented for the past few hours. The biting cold of the dark stone cell had brought on the memory and she had gone with it, lying on the small bunk bed in the cell focusing on how the kids had looked in their brightly colored suits, how they had laughed with every fall, and the feelings she enjoyed when she had been with them. Her memory was strong enough that she could even pull up the smells of the fresh air and the pine trees. If she ever made it out of here alive she would take the kids back to that same resort for a vacation.

She was about to start the day over, replaying it

one more time in her mind like a favorite movie, when the door to the cell snapped open with a bang.

"Don't you ever knock?" Joyce said, swinging her feet off her bunk so she could face whoever was coming in.

"Let's go," a rough voice said as light flooded the small room forcing Joyce to cover her eyes for a moment. Before her vision could completely adjust rough hands pulled her from the bunk and half shoved her toward the door. She couldn't see the guy, but he smelled like he needed a shower and had been eating too much garlic, a stiff combination.

"I can walk," she said, twisting from his grip and stepping away from him.

She moved toward the open door, keeping her pace slow ahead of the guard to give her eyes enough time to adjust.

There looked to be only two of them: the smelly one who had come into the cell and another who stood just outside in the corridor, automatic rifle cocked and aimed right at her stomach. Both men were slightly taller than she was and dressed in the standard green uniform of Larson's goons.

When she reached the corridor she got a better look at both of them. The one in the hall had slicked-back black hair and blue eyes, enhanced, it appeared, by contact lenses. The one who smelled bad had greasy brown hair, a scar on his right cheek, and a potbelly. He looked downright mean through and through.

"Where we heading?" she asked as she stepped

into the corridor and the black-haired guard indicated with his gun that she turn left.

"Nowhere without these tied," the other guard said. He grabbed her hands and yanked them behind her back, pulling a cord around them and yanking it tight.

"Take it easy," she said as the cord cut into her wrists and her shoulders strained backward. "I'm not a piece of meat."

"You are to us," Garlic-breath said and laughed. He let his hands run over her ass, then up her sides toward her breasts.

"Shit, Carl. Cut it out. You don't want Larson pissed, do you?"

"Just having a little fun is all," Garlic-breath said and pushed her roughly to the left. They flanked her, forcing her to move between them toward a cross corridor to the left of her cell. It took her just a moment to realize that the only thing in that direction was the alien sector. She had no doubt she was going to be meeting bugs in very short order and that thought scared the hell out of her.

"You don't have to do this," she said, trying to slow down, give herself some time to think.

"Keep moving," the black-haired guard said and, with a firm grip on her arm, pushed her slightly ahead.

"Kleist's insane," she said, focusing her attention on the guard on the left. He seemed to be the most likely to listen to reason. "You know that. If we work together we can stop him. No more killing."

"Shut up," Garlic-breath said and squeezed her

arm even harder. "Just shut up before I shut you up."

"Wow, that's original," Joyce said.

The intersection of two corridors was coming up and no one else was in sight, at least as far as she could see. There was no doubt she was running out of time. She had to act now.

"You're sure," she asked, again slowing down her pace, "that you want to kill me? I'm a nice person, honest."

With no answer from either of them except to push her forward again, it was time. Move now or she'd be facing bugs and even facing Garlic-breath here was a giant step above that option.

"You know," she said, turning slightly to face Garlic-breath, "didn't anyone ever tell you that you needed a bath?"

With a sudden twist she broke the grip of Garlic-breath and knocked him hard into the stone wall. His gun clattered to the floor. With a quick movement she landed a direct kick on the black-haired guard's chest pounding him back into the opposite wall.

She spun on Garlic-breath. Before he could even climb to his feet she kicked him as hard as she could directly in the crotch. She could feel her foot sink in deep.

He screamed and fell to the floor. She doubted if he'd be walking anytime soon. Couldn't have happened to a nicer guy.

With five quick running strides, her hands tied and flopping behind her back, she was down the hall and around the corner, but she knew this wasn't going to work. She could already hear the black-haired guard climbing to his feet and starting after her. With her hands tied she couldn't even quickly open a goddamned door.

"Joyce!"

The voice sounded familiar, but she didn't know from where and she didn't want to stop at the moment to chat.

"Joyce, damn it! Duck!"

Now she knew the voice. It was Hank's. She flung herself sideways and down as shots cut the air where she had been a moment before. She tumbled head over heels and ended up on her stomach, facing back in the direction she had just come.

Behind her both guards twisted in the air as red holes appeared on their green uniforms. Blood splattered the walls around them as they tumbled to the floor.

Joyce lay on her stomach on the cold stone, breathing hard, watching the life drain out of the two men who had been taking her to her death only a moment before. Her only thought was that she must not have kicked Garlic-breath as hard as she thought she had. Either that or he had nuts of stone.

Then someone was kneeling beside her, working quickly to untie her hands.

"You all right?" Hank said as he finished with the bonds and helped her to her feet.

"I am now," she said. She gave him a hard hug, then nodded to the other red-haired man who stood beside them.

"Kent," Hank said, smiling, "this is Joyce. Joyce. Kent."

"My pleasure, Kent," Joyce said, grabbing the red-haired man's hand and shaking it. "And thanks."

"No, *my* pleasure," he said, laughing at the craziness of the situation. "Anytime."

"Let's hope it's not too often," Joyce said.

"Well," Hank said, glancing quickly around the hall and then pointing to the obvious camera near the ceiling. "It seems we have started the revolution and won the first battle. Shall we retreat?"

"With pleasure," Joyce said. "But first I need a little firepower." She moved quickly to the two dead guards, took both ammunition belts and then picked up both automatic rifles. She slung one over her shoulder and the other she cradled in her arm after quickly checking to make sure it was loaded and ready.

Then she kicked the very dead body of Garlic-breath as hard as she could in the crotch. "That'll teach you to stay down when I kick you the first time."

Hank laughed. "See what I mean, Kent?"

Kent's laugh was hard and long as he ducked through an open ventilation grate in the corridor wall. Hank was right behind him, still laughing.

"Hang on there a minute," Joyce said as she followed them into the dark, narrow ventilation tunnel. "Just what did you mean by that? And what's so funny?"

In the dark in front of her both men laughed even harder.

The Professor watched the huge alien finish devouring the human torso he had just supplied and felt like a proud parent watching his child take its first steps. But this was no normal child. This alien seemed to fill the entire area behind the reinforced window. One clawed hand was bigger than the Professor's entire body, and the jet-black head and huge carapace were larger than some cars. Saliva ran from its huge jaws. With two bites the man's torso was devoured, leaving only a few bloody specks in the pools of alien saliva on the floor. The Professor could hear the faint cracks as the human bones were broken and swallowed.

Kleist clapped his hands together like he was applauding a great stage play. He had done it. He had created the greatest creature in the galaxy. A male alien the size of a queen, maybe even bigger.

And, he hoped, totally tame.

His experiments should have removed all desire to breed or mate from the huge creature. With all matriarchal ties removed and the overwhelming desire to breed removed, the innate ferocity becomes redundant and therefore should also be gone. That was the theory, his theory. He had been right about its size, but was it truly tame?

"Time for the first test," the Professor said. He turned to a control board in front of the window and punched a key. "Is our guest ready?"

Larson's voice came back through the speaker. "Yes, sir."

"Then stand clear," the Professor said, then waited for a moment before punching up a quick sequence of key strokes.

Bright lights filled the area around the huge alien while huge doors clamped down blocking the alien's retreat into the back areas of the alien's pen. The alien reared, startled, its tail swishing back and forth on the floor as it glanced around. It was clearly agitated. Good. That would make this an even better test.

Almost simultaneously with the large doors closing a small, human-sized door slid open on the far wall. A large chair with a human form strapped to it slid on smooth tracks into the very center of the room, jerking to a stop almost quicker than the alien could react.

The Professor noted that the alien hovered over the chair but didn't attack it. Good.

He keyed the microphone for the pen and spoke into it. "Greetings, Mr. Cray. I'd like you to meet my pride and joy."

The alien leaned its huge head down directly in front of Cray's eyes.

All Cray could do was stare in terror as, behind the protective glass, the Professor applauded.

"Sarge," Lynch whispered as he knelt down beside where Green was sitting on the stone plug. The ventilation tunnels flickered in the faint light from Marine lanterns, and distant whispers of men talking filled the air.

Green took a moment to finish planning their next moves after they made it through the blocked passage. Their first chore was to get live ammunition, then slowly but surely start taking out the Professor's guards in a guerrilla action, hitting and pulling back and then hitting again. With Larson having over a hundred men and there only being twenty of them, it would be the only type of fight they could win. Eventually they would reach the Professor. Green didn't know exactly how they would manage that, but he had a few ideas. He sighed and then glanced at Lynch with a nod that he should go ahead.

"Robinsen has an idea that I think might work, if we're lucky." Lynch held his ammunition belt away from his chest. "We dumped the blanks from the rifles, but our belts are still full. These blanks have a good supply of power in them. We should be able to fashion a few quick bombs, at least one that would be big enough to knock the cork out of this." Lynch tapped the huge stone plug that Green was sitting on.

"And how do we slow the bugs down," Green asked, pointing below, "when they follow us right on down there?"

"That's the tricky part," Lynch said, sitting back on his heels and taking a deep breath. "After we've blown open this hole and we're through it, we should be able to cram stuff in the open hole behind us, at least enough to make the blockage solid enough to hold some falling rock from above." Lynch pointed overhead. "We set off two more explosives that will cave in that roof up there and the debris will fill the hole we make with the first blast. No hole, no aliens."

Green glanced up at the ceiling where Lynch had pointed. That might work if they set the bombs right. He could see some structural cracks in the rocks that, with enough explosive, would cave in this entire area.

"The trick," Lynch said, "will be after the first explosion opens the hole. We've got to get down there fast, get the hole blocked with some sort of support, then set off the other two explosions to cave in the roof before the bugs swarm the place."

"How long will it take to pull off?" Green asked.

"Fifteen minutes to fashion and place the bombs. We'll use canteens for the bombs, but the time comes in opening enough of these blank shells for the powder. Then three minutes between explosions, tops."

Green looked around at the men and then down at the sealed passage. He nodded. "Make an extra explosive charge in case the first one doesn't punch through. If we don't use it, we can always toss it at some bugs or maybe some of the Professor's men."

"Will do." Lynch started to move, but Green touched his arm.

"Quietly," Green said. "And fast. We may not have fifteen minutes."

10

The choking smell of the huge alien almost blacked Cray out, but the sheer terror of having something that big, that ugly, that nightmarish, within a few feet of him kept his eyes riveted open and his muscles frozen.

He was still tied to the chair and could barely remember the grilling Larson had given him after threatening him with the face-hugger. The stupid politics of the corporations seemed to carry little weight when faced with wearing one of those. He'd seen pictures of alien births and had prayed many nights that it hadn't happened to Linda, that she had died before implantation.

The huge alien leaned in closer to Cray, as if studying him. The alien's head was far bigger than

Cray's entire body. It extended its interior jaw slowly toward him, like a giant tongue wanting to taste him. The sharp, glistening teeth on the end were all Cray could see. The razor teeth of the small jaw and the huge arm-length teeth of the main jaw became his total world as that huge mouth loomed over him.

Saliva dripped on Cray's left arm, burning the skin. Cray could smell his own sizzling flesh mixed with the overwhelming stink of the alien.

But total paralyzing fear kept Cray perfectly still.

All of his training was gone. He couldn't even bring Linda's face into his memory. All he could do was stare into the huge black throat.

And those razor-sharp teeth.

A small voice in the back of his head fought for his control training, fought for the picture of Linda, of her beautiful face. Anything to leave this reality. But this was too much.

The alien retracted its inner jaws and closed its mouth, the sound of teeth and shell clicking echoing in the room.

Finally the creature backed away slightly and Clay let out the air he'd been holding very slowly. The pain from the acid that had dropped on his arms and leg and the sweat off his forehead were blurring his vision. In the background Cray could hear the Professor talking, but his words meant little to him.

"Isn't he a wonderful creature, Mr. Cray? One of the greatest of all creation, don't you think?"

Cray didn't move as the alien lumbered around him, staring at him, choking him with a thick stench so bad that Cray felt like retching. But he didn't dare.

Once the huge tail brushed the edge of the chair, rocking it almost off its track. Again Cray didn't make the slightest move in the straps that held him. He was nothing more than part of the chair.

The alien again leaned in close, the jaws coming down within a meter of Cray's face, then backing away.

Slowly what was left of the sane part of Cray's brain began to question.

Why was he still alive? Maybe his lack of movement was the reason. Was this how his wife had felt? Did she have time to feel this numbing terror?

"Actually, Mr. Cray," the Professor went on over the speaker. "He is part your son, you might say, sharing your DNA from a scraping of tissue taken when you first arrived. Remember when Grace shook your hand? She's very good at getting needed samples like that."

Cray held totally still, not even daring to let his eyes follow the creature as it moved around him.

Kleist went on. "The rest of this wonderful creature's makeup is a cocktail of alien DNA, concentrated human male hormone, and a rather complex biochemical soup that your employers at the Grant Corporation would have killed to get their hands on.'"

A huge alien hand snaked out and one razor-edged claw touched Cray on his bare chest leaving a red cut from his right nipple to his navel. Then the alien withdrew and studied Cray again.

Cray had no choice but to look into those evil

jaws and not acknowledge the intense pain from the cut and from the acid the alien had left in it like salt in an open wound.

Over the speaker the Professor laughed. "It seems, Mr. Cray, that your son is interested in getting his hands on you. But I don't think he will. You see, I think I have succeeded in finally breeding the first tame alien male. Wonderful, isn't he?"

Cray didn't move, didn't say a word, but in his mind he was shouting: *Tame? Tame? This creature looming over him was far from tame. This creature was pure evil.* But Cray didn't even blink and said nothing out loud and the huge alien continued to hover over him.

After a moment the Professor said, "It seems that this experiment is a total success. Congratulations, Mr. Cray. It seems your son likes you enough to let you live."

The Professor laughed just loud enough for it to come over the speaker, then said, "I, on the other hand, am not nearly so beneficent, as you will soon discover."

The chair jerked hard, tossing Cray against the straps. Accelerating, it slid backward out of the room, again before the huge alien could react.

The last sight Cray had of the creature was its first tentative step toward him as the door closed. It looked angry and very hungry, and not at all happy that it had been tricked.

He prayed to every god he knew as the chair came to a halt that it would be the last time he would ever see that thing.

*   *   *

Sergeant Green had his men spread out in two groups on both sides of the coming explosion. Half were around the corner of the tunnel intersection to the left and half around the corner to the right. The concussion from the explosion in these close quarters was going to be rough. But with a little distance, a little luck, and a few intersections of tunnels to take off the pressure, they would survive.

Now it was just he and Lynch standing over the plugged hole.

He checked the jury-rigged bomb one more time. The explosives were rigged and in place with a ten-second delay on the trigger. When he clicked the trigger, he was to go to the right and Lynch to the left. If the explosion collapsed the entire tunnel they were to each take the men they had with them and run in opposite directions, trying again as soon as possible to break out of the alien sector and into the abandoned tunnels below. Each of them carried two more jury-rigged bombs.

"Ready?" the sergeant asked Lynch. He looked over at the dust-stained and sweating face of his friend and second in command.

Lynch glanced down the tunnel in the direction he would be running, then back at Green. "As I'll ever be. Let's do it."

"Let's hope this works," Green said as he leaned over the bomb. "Be ready to get your ass back here and plant the new charges if it does."

"No sweat," Lynch said.

"Go," Green said. He triggered the ten-second timer, and took off at a full run. He had barely

made the corner and tumbled out of the direct
line of the blast when the bomb went off.

It felt as if someone had put his head inside a
small metal bucket, then smashed it from all sides
at once. His ears rang in a high-pitched wail, and
his head instantly ached as the pressure changed.

A sudden hurricane of dust from every nook
and crack filled the air of the intersection, reduc-
ing visibility to nothing in an instant. He held his
breath, letting some of the dust settle before trying to breathe again.

The shock wave buzzed against his palms on
the stone floor, and then the rumble of falling
rocks could be heard from down the tunnel. God
he hoped that wasn't rock from above blocking
the entire area. That was one of the risks they
were taking, but if it happened he knew they
wouldn't stand a chance in two separate groups.

Hell, they didn't stand much of a chance now
seeing as they had called every alien in the sector
to come down for dinner.

He rolled to his feet and moved his neck and
jaw in an attempt to clear the pressure in his ears.
Through the dust he could see a few of his men
scrambling to their feet. "Be careful as you move
around," he shouted, his voice sounding hollow in
his ringing ears. "I don't want anyone falling down
a damn shaft."

He glanced around at the few men he could
see. "Let's move." He started at a slow run back in
the direction he had just come.

It was like running into a blinding snowstorm.
The gray dust filled the air and ate the beam of his
light within a foot of his head. The dust instantly
coated his face and nose and he had to keep swal-

lowing just to keep his throat clear enough to breathe.

He felt his way along the wall with one hand on the cold stone, moving as quickly as he could. Behind him he could hear his men doing the same.

He reached the intersection and suddenly the air seemed slightly clearer. A draft was pulling the dust down through the new hole they had punched where the sealed shaft had been a minute before. The hole was rough, but not so large that they couldn't plug it with supports that would hold the falling rock from a second explosion.

Lynch appeared out of the dust on the other side of the intersection, a rope in one hand and a light in the other.

"Let's go!" Green shouted. "Set the new charges and make sure that plug is the right size." Two men instantly went up the stone ladder above the shaft to plant the charges. Two others pulled the equipment they had tied together to make a plug closer to the hole and started some quick measuring. The plug was made up of rifles for support tied with rope and supported with other standard equipment such as shovels and climbing gear from their packs.

Green grabbed the rope off his belt and dropped it through the hole, swinging it over his shoulder and under his arm. He spread his legs and braced himself. Lynch quickly followed on the other side of the hole. Then, with Green and Lynch holding the upper ends, the men were quickly through and down to the lower levels, including the two who had set the explosives in the passageway and ceiling above them.

"All set?" Green asked Lynch, glancing through

the dust at where the explosives were placed above.

"Enough to bring the whole section down," Lynch said. "One-minute timer rigged out of my watch and secured on the wall."

Green took the rope from Lynch's hand and dropped both through the hole to the men waiting on the level below. Then he quickly stepped over to the trigger dangling from a wire down one stone wall.

"Plug ready?" They were going to need something blocking the hole that was strong enough to hold the falling rock from above. Otherwise there was a chance that the rock they were going to blast from the ceiling would just go right on down the shaft, leaving it open for the bugs to follow.

Lynch pulled the mass of tied equipment a few inches closer to the hole. He pulled and twisted at it, then glanced up at Green. "It'll work," he said. "Open enough to let the blast through, but strong enough to hold all the first rocks that hit it. I just hate leaving the rifles." He patted one that was tied into the plug.

"No choice. Let's do it before we get unwanted company."

He clicked the timer. One minute and counting.

With two quick steps he was at the hole and on his stomach working his way over the edge of the rough blast crater. Lynch snapped off his light and tucked it in his belt. Green left his light on the edge shining down into the hole. Below them one of the men had left a light shining upward so that they had at least dim light to work in.

On the opposite side of the hole Lynch was

lowering himself over the edge at exactly the
same time until his back touched Green's.

They paused for a moment, making sure their
backs were square, their legs braced against the
rough stone, and the pressure as even as they
could get it between them. There were handholds
in the side of the stone down about ten feet,
carved there by the prisoners, but the blast had
blown the others above it away. They had to get
to the stone ladder, as well as seal the hole as
they went. Back to back down the hole was the
quickest and safest way and something they had
practiced at times over the years.

Green scraped his knees and hands on the
sharp rock as he went, and after a few seconds he
could feel blood start to run down his right leg.

But quickly they had their heads below the top
of the hole.

"Pull it over," Green said.

Lynch quickly and smoothly scraped the mass
of equipment that would serve as a new plug over
the edge and down on top of them. Using one
hand each to work the plug down and the other
hand and both legs to hold themselves in place,
they continued down the hole until the equipment
snuggled into place about three feet from the top.

"Got it," Lynch said.

"Make sure," Green said. Both he and Lynch
pulled and tugged on it, almost hanging their total
weight on it to make sure it was secure.

"Twenty-six seconds," Green said as they finished securing the plug and started down again.
He reached the cut handholds on his side and
with one arm swung Lynch around so that he too

had a firm grasp. Lynch started down, then suddenly paused and sniffed.

But Green had already caught the familiar odor of rotten eggs that filled the dusty, dry air of the dark tunnels.

"Aliens," Green said. "Go! Go! Go!"

Like two monkeys the men scrambled ten more feet down the wall and then dropped the rest of the way to the stone floor, both barely missing the vertical shaft that disappeared off into the dark below the ladder.

"Run for it!" Green said as both men turned to the right and headed down the tunnel through the dust at a full run. The tracks of the other men covered the floor. They had been ordered to get three or four intersections away from the blast in the direction of the human sector and then wait. If he and Lynch didn't make it, the men's orders were to search for and destroy the Professor at all costs.

All the men were secure behind solid rock a hundred meters distant.

A lone flashlight sat in the middle of the corridor ahead, marking the intersection they were trying to reach.

They'd be lucky to make it to that first corner.

The sounds of aliens filling the area above the plug filtered after them as a reminder to run even faster.

Green could feel his heart pumping as he sprinted right behind Lynch toward the promising light.

And for a moment he thought they might make it.

Then the concussion from the huge blast sent

Green flying forward like a giant hand had caught him squarely in the back and just shoved.

He tucked in midair and rolled as best he could. The impact against the stone floor jarred him and snapped his head around as he tumbled, letting his forward motion take up as much of the impact as it could.

After what seemed like a nightmare of pounding noise and spinning rock he finally came to a smashing stop against the wall on the far side of the intersection.

A shooting pain cut through his head, and as the blackness took him his last thought was a silent hope that the hole was sealed, not only by tons of rock, but by a few bug bodies as well.

Joyce sat on the cold stone of the passageway, the comforting feel of the automatic rifle in her hand beside her. She couldn't remember being so cold before, but there was no hope of getting warm soon so she was ignoring it as best she could. But seeing her breath crystallize in front of her every time she breathed didn't help. It also didn't help that all she wore were cloth slacks, a sweat-stained T-shirt, and a cloth vest. A good ski parka right now was what she really needed. And maybe some mittens and a knit hat.

Hank and Kent were talking with four other men over plotting the best way to take out the Professor and his goons. Joyce didn't really care what plan they came up with, as long as it had her pulling the trigger.

The men stood in a circle, their breath misting in the lamplight between them, giving the scene a surreal quality straight out of a black and white movie.

She watched Hank, how he moved his hands when he talked, how he brushed his hair off his face. She was really glad to see him again, to see him alive. Somehow it gave her a warm feeling inside. Not enough to cut the cold of the stone tunnels, but at least it was something.

She heard the name of her ship mentioned a few times and was about to stand and join the discussion when a low rumbling filled the corridor and dust drifted from the walls, giving the lights around them even more of a ghostly look.

She picked up the rifle and studied the shadows in the tunnels around them.

"What the hell was that?" Hank asked as everyone stopped and looked around.

"Maybe," Joyce said, standing and moving over to join the group, "there are more than just us fighting the Professor. Could that be possible?"

"Might be," Hank said, "but more likely it was one of the Professor's experiments gone bad. Could we be so lucky as to have it take him out?"

"I hope not," Joyce said as she calmly adjusted the strap of the rifle over her shoulder with cold fingers. "I don't think the man deserves such an easy death. Something like a face-hugger would be more along the lines I'm thinking."

All the men stopped and looked at her through the dusty light. It was clear to Joyce that they were all thinking their private thoughts of how they would like to see the Professor leave this world. From the slight nods and the looks on their faces, Joyce doubted if any of them seriously disagreed with her.

Finally Hank rested a hand on her shoulder and then broke the uneasy silence. "We have to assume the explosion, or whatever it was, doesn't change a thing."

"Agreed," Kent said and the others, including Joyce, nodded.

"But what we're not agreed on," Hank said, "is what we do next."

Joyce glanced around at the six men, noting that she was by far the best armed of the group. Seven people against Larson and his goons. Larson must have a good hundred men, all armed and ready to die. They didn't stand a chance.

She cleared her throat and stepped forward slightly, forcing Hank's hand to drop off her shoulder. "I'd say the first course of action would be to get more firepower and more help."

She glanced around the dim, dust-filtered light at the others. They all seemed to be agreeing, listening intently to her, willing almost to let her lead. So what the hell. She would.

"I've got a copilot somewhere who's a damn good shot. And the guy Cray, who they caught me with, killed at least two of Larson's men with his bare hands before they got him. He'd be a good addition to our little force if he's still alive."

"I agree," Kent said. "And he's still alive. Or at least he was an hour ago. He's in what serves almost as a holding pen next to the Professor's private labs."

A tall, thin guy dressed in a white shirt and black, dust-covered pants said, "Your copilot left the bar with a blonde about three hours ago. I'll bet he's in his room."

"All right," Joyce said. "Someone give me a

shove in the right direction and a rough map of these tunnels and I'll get those two. Who else can we draft?"

For the next twenty minutes they outlined whom each of them were going after and where they would meet when they finished. Then one at a time the group broke up, scattering in different directions in the dark tunnels until only Joyce and Hank were left.

"You sure you want to go this alone?" Hank asked, his hand a faint touch on her arm, his breath ice crystals in the remaining lamplight.

"Yeah," she said, giving his hand a quick squeeze. "We need all the help we can get. You're going after three recruits. I can manage my two."

He nodded, but Joyce could tell he didn't much like the idea of splitting up with her again. She reached up and grabbed his forearm as tight as her cold fingers would allow. "What'd you tell Kent about me before you two came to my rescue?"

Hank looked puzzled for a moment, then smiled.

"Come on," she said, smiling back at him. "I can take it."

Hank looked down at the ground for a moment, then back into her eyes. "I told him you were a woman who could take care of herself."

She smiled at him, holding his gaze. "Then let me do it," she said.

He smiled back, then nodded. "Two hours?"

"Two hours," she replied. "And you take care of yourself."

"I will," he said.

"Promise?"

"Promise."

She smiled and without another look turned and headed off down the dark tunnel, her small-beamed light cutting a weak line through the blackness.

Cray first, if he was still alive, then Deegan. That was her plan. Cray first because he might not live much longer, then Deegan if she could find him.

It felt good to be doing something.

Real good.

She checked her rifle for the tenth time to make sure it was fully loaded, then slung it over her shoulder. Holding the flashlight in her mouth, she started up the ladder cut into the wall.

Her fingers were numb on the cold rock as she climbed slowly toward the Professor's labs, but she didn't notice. She was hoping to find the Professor alone and get off a shot.

Just one shot. That was all she was asking for.

One shot for Jerry.

11

Sergeant Green awoke to the feeling of a bandage being applied to his right arm. He was leaning against something hard, with sharp edges.

"He's coming around," a voice said. "Back off. Give him some room."

Shadows beyond his closed eyes retreated and suddenly he was bathed in bright light. He blinked against the dust caked on his face and the glare of two lamps shining directly at him.

"Give me a break," he said, using his good arm to shade his face. His head felt like a jet engine was taking off behind his eyes and there was a high-pitched whine in his right ear. He was afraid to move, unwilling to find out how many bones he had broken.

"Sorry, Sarge."

The lights were quickly shifted out of his eyes enough for him to see the dirt-covered faces around him. Private Young stood over him, looking concerned, while Robinsen, kneeling beside him, finished on his arm. Both of their breaths showed in the lamplight as frozen crystals sparkling like a light Christmas snow. Getting out of the alien section of the base had cooled things down in more ways than one.

He started to move, but an intense pain shot through his head. He moaned and slouched back against the wall, wishing someone would just kill him and get it over with.

"You got a good egg there above your right ear," Robinsen said. "Has to hurt like hell."

"Wow," Green said, using his good hand to slowly touch the lump. It was soft, swollen, and felt hot and sticky to his touch. "What a headache."

"You're lucky that's all it is," Robinsen said. "I've given you some Black-Ace for the pain. It should be easing in a few seconds. I don't think you have any broken bones beyond a few cracked ribs and the lump on the head. We'll have to watch you in case that lump is a bad concussion, but I don't think it is."

Green sighed and leaned back against the wall. No broken bones. That, at least, was good news. The last thing he wanted was his men carrying him. He took some deep breaths, feeling the cracked ribs that Robinsen had mentioned. He could feel the wave of Black-Ace cleaning out the aches like a hot shower after a good workout. That was some good shit. The soothing felt so good he just wanted to sleep. He couldn't do that, but he wanted to. Maybe just until Robinsen finished working on his arm.

He closed his eyes to the bright lamps, then immediately opened them again. No sleeping. He could live on these drugs for a while if he needed to. And judging from the pain in his head it looked like he was going to have to. It wouldn't be the first time he'd been hooked on Black-Ace. Damn near every Marine was at one time or another. It was standard issue and they used it, but coming down off the drug was going to be a bitch. He just hoped he lived long enough to worry about it.

He took another two deep breaths of the cold, dust-filled air to help his head clear, then he sat up slowly and glanced around. Only three men were near him at this intersection of corridors. Robinsen working on his cut arm, Young holding the lamps, and McPhillips standing guard before the right-hand tunnel. But he could hear others talking a short distance off.

"That'll do it," Robinsen said, patting the bandage on Green's arm and then standing. Robinsen reached out and offered Green a hand up. Green took it and was gratefully helped to his feet.

He felt dizzy for a moment and leaned against the cold stone wall, but it quickly cleared. The drug was kicking in. Now his head only felt like it had been hit with a bat, not crushed by a truck. It was an improvement. He'd be even better when his ears stopped ringing.

He glanced around at the intersection, then back the way he had come. "I assume," he said, "since we're all just sitting here, that the hole we made is plugged?"

"Totally," Young said. "That was one wail of a blast."

Green nodded. "It took a few bugs with it, too." He clapped his hands together to try to warm them. "Looks like it shut off the heat, as well." Green glanced around, looking at the scattered rock and for the first time really remembering the blast. "Where's Lynch? How's his head?"

The three men around him were silent and none of them looked him directly in the eyes.

He got the message.

"What happened?"

Robinsen pointed at the vertical shaft leading down to the lower levels. "Looks like when the explosion went off you were tossed against the wall and Lynch was unlucky enough to tumble into the shaft. He went down three levels before hanging up on the edge of the hole. His neck was broken, as were about half the bones in his body."

"Damn," was all Green could say. What a stupid thing to happen.

Robinsen and the other men said nothing.

Green walked to the edge of the shaft and glanced down the stone handholds cut in the wall. The hole went into the dark as far as he could see, with faint lights showing three levels below.

He stepped back and took a few deep breaths letting the painkiller work its magic. Everyone in the outfit knew he had been closer to Lynch than any of the other men. He depended on Lynch, had confided in Lynch. Lynch was his second in command.

"Damn it," he said softly, staring at the black

mouth of the shaft. He knew better than to think they were going to get out of this without losing some more.

That was the nature of their business.

That was the nature of war.

But why Lynch after all this time? After surviving all the stupid missions the Professor had sent them on, why die like this? It was just plain stupid.

The Professor was going to suffer for this. And for Choi and Boone and all the others.

He was going to suffer very long and very hard.

Green glanced back at where Robinsen stood quietly. "You're now my number two. Young, you're three. Understood?"

Both nodded.

"We're in a war here and we have a mission," Green said. "If I go down I need you to carry it out. The mission in plain terms is to take out the Professor and Larson and as many of his goons as we can. And do it in as slow and as painful a way as possible. Is that understood?"

"On the money," Robinsen said.

"With pleasure," Young said.

Green nodded, pleased at their responses, but not showing it. "Round up the men and meet three levels down in five minutes."

Young nodded and quickly disappeared down the tunnel. Robinsen followed Green to the edge of the shaft and Green let him go down first.

Professor Kleist was soon going to get a big surprise. He now had nineteen very angry Marines after him. Green knew it wasn't going to be pretty when they finally caught up with him.

And that thought helped him through the pain going down the cold stone ladder.

And through the pain of seeing one of his best men, and his best friend, laid out dead on the cold stone floor three levels below.

Joyce finally had her hands almost warm and was beginning to get some feeling in her feet again when they brought Cray out of the lab across the ten-meter-wide corridor from her. She had been sitting out of sight in a side ventilation shaft, watching the wide, carpeted corridor along the Professor's private labs, waiting to get any indication of where Cray might be. Now, suddenly, he was being pushed along in front of her.

He had on the same brown slacks and tan shirt he had worn earlier, but they were now torn and looked to be bloodstained across his chest and down his right leg.

She watched, staying out of sight behind the ventilation grate in the stone wall as Cray was tossed by Larson and one of his goons into a small room beside one of the Professor's labs. She could tell Cray wasn't doing that well, and from the way they were handling him, it didn't look like he was going to get better much quicker.

Larson checked to make sure the lock was secure, then left a single guard standing in front of Cray's cell while he went back into the main lab toward the Professor's office.

She wished Larson had been alone. She'd have taken him out without a second thought. And if it had been the Professor she would have, even with a dozen men around him. But right now her first

job was to get Cray out of there and to see if he
was going to be of any help to her.

The one guard stood with his back to the door
in parade-rest position. His gun hung on a strap
over his shoulder and he didn't seem to be paying
a great deal of attention. Joyce studied him, thinking of the best ways to get past him. He looked to
be not much older than twenty, with blond hair
and very white skin. He had, what might be called
under the right circumstances, a nice face. In the
bored rest position it seemed almost friendly. And
he looked much cleaner than the two she had
fought with earlier.

Joyce studied him for a minute, giving Larson
plenty of time to get a distance away. She was going to make some noise and she wanted as few
people close as possible. For the last half hour the
corridor had gotten very little traffic. And what
traffic there was seemed to be techs in white lab
coats.

Silently she took the second rifle off her shoulder, checked to make sure it was ready, and then
put it silently back over her shoulder. Her plan
was to take out the guard with one shot from hiding, break open the grate, shoot open the lock on
the door, and then she and Cray would disappear
back into the dark ventilation system before anyone was the wiser. But just in case someone was
too close she wanted the extra gun in Cray's
hands when he came out of that door.

She quickly checked the corridor to make sure
no one was coming, then pushed herself away
from the grate, bracing her back against the stone.
She checked to make sure the rifle was set on single shot, then carefully aimed at the center of the

guard's chest, not looking at his face as she did so. The shot was going to be damn near deafening in this tight place, but firing in the ventilation system would also be an advantage because it would be hell to pinpoint quickly.

She just hoped her ears survived.

She took two slow breaths, and then, keeping the rifle leveled dead center on the guard's chest, moved the barrel of the gun up and through the grate just enough to prevent the bullet deflecting off the metal.

Then she squeezed the trigger.

The concussion bumped her head backward with a sharp knock into the stone. The sound hammered her like her head was in a sleep tank and twenty people were pounding it with steel pipes. The smell made her cough and she did once, hard, before kicking the grate off with her foot. It landed on the carpeted corridor floor with a loud thump that seemed very distant in her ringing ears.

In a smooth motion she clicked her Kramer to fully automatic and did a quick scan of the hall. The guard, a round hole in his chest and a startled look on his face, was slumped over next to the door. A red smear covered the expensive wood paneling behind him.

Before the guard's head hit the floor she was out of the grate and across the corridor. "Cray," she shouted, "stand away from the door!"

She gave him only a second and then sent three shots in a downward angle into the lock. With a hard kick, the door crashed inward.

Cray appeared out of the dark interior like a ghost. He was barefoot and she had been right about the spots on his clothes being blood. He looked to be bleeding from four or five different places, but he seemed to be alert and Joyce was very glad he was moving so quickly. She wouldn't have taken the time to carry him.

With a quick shake of the head, "No" to Joyce as she started to swing the second gun off her shoulder, he bent over and yanked the Kramer off the dead guard, grabbing the extra clips of ammunition and the full combat belt with another quick motion.

Joyce watched for a second, then turned and in four running steps was back at the grate opening.

She was through it in a fraction of a second, with Cray right behind her.

Two hundred meters of ventilation shafts and three levels down, she stopped to catch her breath.

Cray slumped to the floor across the tunnel from her and smiled. "Thanks," he said, his voice raspy.

"Don't thank me yet," she said, working to catch her breath. Now she was hot and sweating, which felt wonderful compared to freezing. "We're outnumbered about thirty to one and the fight looks impossible."

He laughed, almost a high, insane laugh. "If you'd seen what I have in the last few hours, you'd be glad you even have the chance to fight. So thanks."

She looked at him, at the blood splattered over his shirt, at the red and purple areas of his face. He had obviously been through hell. Maybe, like her, he'd want a little payback.

"You're welcome," she said.

He smiled and closed his eyes. She'd give him ten minutes of rest and then they had another person to draft.

Kleist glanced away from the window looking over his creation when Grace entered his private lab. He was angrier than he had been in years. He hated incompetence and it seemed to be all around him. Moreover, he hated being wrong and his creature had just proved him very, very wrong.

He kept his voice as calm as he could and asked, "Have they found him yet?"

"No, sir," Grace said. "There would seem to be at least ten and maybe as many as twenty people involved so far, all seemingly heavily armed. Besides Cray's release, there have been six incidents on the station in the last hour. We have four men dead at this point and two wounded."

"Find Cray and Palmer and bring them to me," the Professor said and turned back to the carnage beyond the reinforced window. He stared at his beautiful creation as it tore a normal-sized alien male apart with a ferocity he found hard to imagine. The body of the adult male smashed against the wall, acid blood splattering everywhere.

"I've been a fool, Grace. A complete fool."

"You're being too hard on yourself," Grace said.

The Professor gestured at the mess beyond the window. "No, I'm not. In my conceit, I overlooked the obvious. I ignored the primary fundamentals of nature. I imagined they wouldn't apply to this unique strain. But, as is now clearly obvious, I was wrong. Wrong, Grace. Wrong. Do you understand?"

She said nothing and they both continued to watch the destruction.

Of the ten mature adult aliens he had let into the contained area with his new creation, only two remained. And as he and Grace watched, one was picked up like it was a light snack, its head bitten completely through. Then the body was tossed in an acid smear against the window in front of them. Before the last survivor had a chance to even run, the huge alien was on it, tearing its arms off first, then its legs, and finally its head, adding its body to the pile of others.

The Professor turned his back on the window and walked a few steps away. "Don't you see, Grace? The alien king refrained from attacking Cray not because its natural savagery had been bred out, as I thought, but because Cray was strapped down, incapacitated, not moving."

Kleist glanced up into Grace's beautiful android face. "Don't you see?" He so wanted someone to understand. "Cray was spared because he wasn't perceived as a threat."

He turned back to the window beyond which the huge alien was smashing the remains of its ten smaller cousins. Cousins who could kill ten men without a problem were now tossed aside like a child's broken toys.

He stood there for a moment, staring at the destruction. Then slowly he smiled. "Maybe it's just a matter of perspective."

"Perspective, Professor?" Grace asked, moving to stand beside him in front of the bloody scene.

"What we have here"—the Professor indicated the huge alien beyond the wall—"is in essence a rogue male. He's a living engine of destruction, the exact opposite of what I had planned for. He considers all others to be his rivals."

"That would seem to be obvious, now," Grace said as the rogue picked up a large piece of another alien and savagely smashed it against the wall.

"Don't you see, Grace?" The Professor was now beaming.

On the other side of the glass the huge alien rose on its hind legs and opened its mouth like it was screaming in celebration of its victory.

"Don't you see? This is the perfect prototype for Z.C.T. Corporation's bio-weapons arsenal. From the ashes of defeat come success."

Grace was about to say something when suddenly she put her hand to the side of her head and looked off into the distance.

"Is something wrong?" the Professor asked.

"Professor, I've just picked up two transmission signals on the upper EF band. To my knowledge we have no facilities for broadcasting on that frequency."

The Professor glanced at the rogue as it stood in the center of its victory, its huge mouth open in a silent scream.

"Can you trace their source?"

Grace nodded, her hand still beside her head as if she had a headache. "One is on this level, in the very heart of the alien sector."

"And the other?" the Professor asked, already knowing the answer.

"From there," Grace said, and pointed at the rogue.

"A challenge," the Professor said softly, and then smiled.

His rogue was challenging the queen.

This might turn out much better than he had ever dreamed. Much better, indeed.

12

With a small map in one hand and a penlight in the other, Joyce led Cray up a series of dark, narrow ventilation shafts cut through solid stone. It seemed like it had been an eternity since Hank and Kent had rescued her. She was starting to memorize the maze of ventilation shafts and tunnels that surrounded the main corridors of the human sector. She had a natural sense of direction, and almost instinctively knew which tunnel would take them where. She had a sneaking feeling that sense was going to come in real handy before all this was over.

Cray, on the other hand, still seemed in shock. Whatever the Professor and Larson had done to him had affected him at a very deep level. He wasn't the same man who had arrived here such a short number of days before. Instead of cocky and sure of himself, a man walking tall and confident into any situation, he now moved like he was afraid of every shadow, hunched slightly forward, almost cowering.

And when he glanced at her, his eyes didn't seem to actually see her, but instead some vision he didn't want to witness again but couldn't shake. She had seen that look in people's eyes a number of times during the war and she would never get used to it.

At one intersection she stopped and turned to Cray. "How you doing?" she whispered.

"Besides feeling like a lost gopher?" he said. "Fine."

She patted his leg and motioned for them to keep moving.

Twice in the next few minutes they found themselves crawling on their stomachs, the weight of meters of rock pressing down on their backs, their rifles pushed ahead of them in the dust.

A few minutes later at one intersection of larger ventilation ducts they were almost surprised by two of Larson's guards crouched in the dark. If one of the guards hadn't tapped his gun against the floor as they approached they might have been dead. Instead of getting into a fight in such close quarters, Cray and Joyce had silently worked their way back and around another way, climbing up two levels to avoid that area.

Finally, after almost an hour of silent and steady movement, they were at their destination. Or at least Joyce hoped it was Deegan's room vent. She motioned for Cray to be quiet and guard her back, then she handed him her rifle and got down on her hands and knees. In this area the vents were near the ceilings of the rooms, but on the floors of the tunnels.

The vent itself was small, not more than a meter wide, two thirds of a meter tall and two meters long. And it was far from smooth rock on the four surfaces. She could feel rough edges scrape against her back as she eased forward to the grate and air filter into the room.

Through it she could see some of the room including Deegan's favorite jacket and his hat tossed on the dresser. This was his room all right.

She could also hear some low moaning, like someone was hurt or had been beaten. Her stomach twisted. Maybe Larson had already been here and had tortured Deegan looking for her. She wouldn't put that past Larson or the Professor.

She backed silently out of the tunnel with only a slight scrape on one elbow and stood to face Cray. "He might be hurt in there, or there may be someone with him. Can't tell, but I'm going in."

She didn't wait for Cray to respond She turned and glanced at the small vent again. If she worked it right she could get the surprise on whoever was holding Deegan. But it would have to be a timed and very fast movement. Otherwise she was dead and in that tight a space there would be very little Cray could do to help her.

She turned back and again whispered in his ear, "I'm going in feetfirst. You come in behind me headfirst and cover me from the vent. If I'm captured or killed, make a run for it."

He nodded that he understood what she was planning. She could see him taking deep breaths, fighting to push back whatever demons were plaguing him. She appreciated that. Maybe there was hope for him yet.

She handed her rifle to him again and then laid down on the floor scooting silently into the tunnel feetfirst. She could feel the dust and dirt bunching up under her shirt and vest. The sharp edges of rock scraped lines in her skin. She refused to focus on the rock walls of the small vent. It had already flashed through her mind once too many times how this looked and felt very much like a coffin.

When she was in position Cray handed her back her rifle.

With a quick nod she indicated to him that she was ready.

She took a deep, silent breath, and then with a violent kick sent the screen flying into the room.

The crash of her foot kicking the grate sounded like a bomb going off. But almost before the screen could hit the floor in Deegan's room, she had slid forward and dropped to the ground, crouched, ready to fire. Behind and above her Cray came through the tunnel face-first, rifle also ready.

In the bed a very surprised and very nude Deegan sat up, his eyes round and his hands above his head. An equally nude blond woman sat up beside him, her hands also shooting above her head in the traditional sign of surrender. Her eyes were bigger around than Deegan's, but Deegan looked more like he was going to choke.

Joyce glanced quickly around the small room to make sure no one was hiding anywhere, then went quickly to the door to make sure it was locked.

In the vent above her head Cray chuckled.

Finally Deegan swallowed hard, and with a glance up at Cray sticking out of the vent, he looked back at Joyce. "Jesus, boss. You could at least knock."

Cray snorted and Joyce laughed, some of the tension easing from her shoulders and back. It was good to be back with Deegan. She hadn't realized just how much she had been worrying about him.

"I'll guard the passage," Cray said. "Be quick. They know we're here by now."

"Thirty seconds," Joyce said to Deegan, "and then we leave you to Larson's goons."

"What the . . ." Deegan started to say.

Joyce grabbed Deegan's old shirt off the floor and tossed it his way. "Twenty-nine. And I'm not kidding."

Joyce turned to the blonde who, from the look in her green eyes, was about to go into total shock. "If you know how to fire one of these"— Joyce held up her automatic Kramer—"you can come along. Otherwise you might want to get dressed very quickly. I suspect you will be having some company from Larson and his goons very, very shortly. And from my experience they don't treat women very well."

The woman choked and jumped from her side of the bed at the same time as Deegan was out the other. Without a glance back she bolted for the door. But Joyce beat her to it, holding it closed.

"You forgot your clothes," she pointed out. "Be-

sides, we need to be out of here"—Joyce pointed
to the open vent—"before you go out there. Understood?"

The woman nodded, her face so pale she almost looked like a ghost.

"Get dressed," Joyce told her, then turned to
see that Deegan was finishing with the buckle on
his pants and had already tossed his boots
through the vent.

"Give me a boost," he said.

Joyce moved quickly into position, cupped her
hands, and then lifted, watching as Deegan forced
his overweight body through the narrow vent. It
must have really hurt. Next trip she'd force him to
lose a little of that weight.

If there was a next trip.

"Nice meeting you," she said to the stunned
woman who stood with a gold blouse in one hand
not even attempting to cover her chest or thick
blond pubic hair. Joyce made a second mental
note to talk to Deegan about his choice of women.

As she heard running outside in the hall, she
turned and pulled herself up and through the duct.

They were already to the first cross vent and
going up a level when she heard Deegan's door
crash open.

That poor blond woman was not having a very
good day.

With the upcoming fight with the Professor and
Larson's men, Sergeant Green could see no other
option but to leave Lynch's body near where he
died. They had found an area where fifty bunks

were dug into the side of the wall of one tunnel. Two bodies of prisoners, mummified by the dry, cold air, rested in two of the upper bunks. Green had the men put Lynch into a middle bunk about chest high off the floor.

Green had arranged him so that he looked peaceful, his gun gripped in his hands in front of his chest along with the picture of his dead wife, Karen, that he had always carried in his wallet. Just like Green's wife, Marybeth, she'd been taken by the aliens in the invasion of Earth. He and Lynch had killed a lot of bugs over the years to make up for those two human deaths.

Green put a light over the bunk and then, without words, all the men filed silently past and moved off down the tunnel toward the human section. Some touched Lynch lightly on the arm to say good-bye.

A few saluted

Young left a small gold pin on his chest.

Green was the last to pass and he stopped for a moment. He patted his old friend's arm. "I'll try to come back for you," he said, "when we finish the mission. You'll be safe here."

He glanced around at the dark tunnel and then back at his friend. "If I don't make it, I suppose we'll both know about it together, upstairs, huh?"

He took a deep, almost shuddering breath. "Going to miss you. Say hi to Karen for me. And to Marybeth, if you see her."

He stood for a moment, not knowing what else to say. Neither he nor Lynch had a religious bone in their bodies so even a short prayer seemed just plain wrong.

He adjusted his rifle on his shoulder, shifting the weight. "See you, old friend."

He picked up the light and moved off quickly down the dark tunnel after his men. They had a fight to fight.

One they were going to damn well win.

The Professor's office was deadly silent as Larson and Grace stood behind Kleist and all three watched the four center screens on the wall play the same event from four different angles.

Finally Larson said, after rerunning the recording of what occurred in Captain Palmer's copilot's quarters, "They're using the damn ventilation system like a highway."

The Professor turned to Larson. He was getting angrier by the minute. Not so much because of the escape of Cray and Palmer and the small insurrection by a few malcontents. That actually didn't bother him beyond annoyance. It was something he had been expecting and now wasn't in the slightest surprised that Captain Palmer had triggered it.

No, what bothered him the most was Larson's apparent inability to handle the situation. The Professor had put up with a lot from his chief of security, but he had thought he had the man fully trained and ready for this. But now the idiot was letting them all down.

And Kleist hated it when people let him down.

"So what have you done about it?" the Professor asked. "At the moment I have much more important matters to attend to. Do you realize that I have just made a breakthrough of unparalleled importance in the lab?" The Professor glanced at Larson's blank face. "No, of course you don't. But I have. For your information, I have just created the ultimate fighting machine. And what is my reward for such an achievement?" He gestured at the screens in front of him in disgust. "I find myself dealing with your petty problems."

He looked Larson directly in the eye. "Do you understand what I'm saying?"

Larson swallowed and nodded. "Yes, sir."

"Fine," the Professor said. He swung back and faced the wall of monitors, his fingers steepled in front of him. "Now show me what you are doing to remedy the situation. And be quick about it."

Larson leaned over the board and punched a few keys. The center four screens of the huge wall displayed a large map of the main level of the human sector. Larson punched another key and blue lines appeared lacing the map through the walls and thick areas around rooms. It was a view the Professor had never seen before and it shocked him.

"This shows the ventilation system that we have mapped from the very poor records left us when they redid this place. There are many more ventilation and service tunnels than this, but at the moment we are working off this layout."

Damn. He should have had those tunnels mapped in the first year. He had no idea there were so many of them. How, with his work with the aliens, was he supposed to think of things like this? He nodded to Larson to continue.

"I've got men stationed at all the major ventilation tunnel intersections on this level, as well as the ones above and below it. They've heard movement, but so far no contact."

"Double the normal guard on the lab areas."

"Already done," Larson said. "And I have men on every person we have suspected in the past of anticorporation activities. At least the ones we can find. At this point we have about twenty missing."

The Professor nodded. "All right. And you figure all of them have joined Cray and Captain Palmer?"

"I'm afraid so," Larson said. "If we don't flush them from the ventilation shafts pretty soon, I'll take a force down into the lower tunnels with motion and heat sensors. These ventilation shafts all empty directly into the tunnels below, so they won't be able to hide for long."

The Professor studied the map of ventilation tunnels for a moment, then said, "A good plan. Check with me before you start the operation in the tunnels."

"Yes, sir."

"Now," the Professor asked. He'd been looking forward to this next question. "Show me what happened to our friendly Marines?"

Again Larson's fingers tapped over the control board beside the Professor and the center four screens changed to a map of the main level of the alien sector.

"Looks like the aliens took the first group of them here." Larson indicated the dots on the map of the tracers in the helmets and on the armor. "They haven't moved, so I assume they're dead."

The Professor shuddered. No! This couldn't be

happening. Larson could not really be this stupid. But he didn't say anything. He just waited for Larson to continue, the sinking feeling in his stomach growing by the second. It was a feeling that this was going to take a great deal more of his attention than he had hoped it would.

Larson punched another two keys and the map was replaced by another, two levels down. "They lost a few more here."

He brought up a third and a fourth map of the next levels down. "And the last ones here and here, including Green. Your plan worked, sir. They're all dead and accounted for."

The Professor stared at the map for a moment, then slowly swung around to face Larson. He couldn't believe what he had seen on those screens or the stupidity of his second in command. This total incompetence was going to drive him crazy. As soon as this entire event was calmed down and Cray recovered and killed, he would find a replacement for Larson. The man was just too stupid to let live.

"Nice job, sir," Larson said, still looking up at the screen. Then he looked down at his boss and his eyes widened.

The Professor smiled at the sudden look of fear flashing in Larson's eyes. He enjoyed that look in the people around him. He could trust people who feared him.

"How long has it been since those bodies were supposedly killed?"

Larson glanced nervously up at the screen, still not understanding what the Professor was talking about. That was the problem with Larson. He just hadn't spent enough time with the aliens. The Professor would soon fix that. Very soon.

"About three hours," Larson said.

"And, Mr. Larson, in your limited knowledge of the aliens, what do they do with humans they capture? Why are we always giving them live humans?"

Larson swallowed and kept his gaze locked on the board. "They, uh . . . they implant them and hang them on the wall in the chambers around the queen?"

"Very good," the Professor said in his best schoolteacher voice. "And do they ever just hang them any old place, such as where they find them?"

"No, they usually—" Larson turned suddenly white as he realized his mistake. "The Marines spotted the tracers and dumped them?"

"Now you've got it." The Professor applauded and Larson's face turned even whiter. "But one more question. If you were Sergeant Green, unarmed and stranded on that side of the alien sector, how would you try to escape? Now granted, I'm not saying you're as smart as Green, but just this once try to think like him."

Larson looked at the screens full of maps for a moment, then reached over and punched up a cross section of the alien section. There were at least ten levels of tunnels below the sealed-off alien section. "I'd try to get down into there," Larson said. Then he looked at the Professor, a real look of panic now crossing his face. "The explosions? You think they made it through?"

The Professor nodded, staring back at the cross section of the alien sector. "I'd say, Mr. Larson, that you might want to prepare your men for a Marine invasion."

Then the Professor laughed. "And if I know Sergeant Green, he's going to be as mad as that rogue I have in the other room."

13

It took Joyce, Deegan, and Cray a full hour from leaving Deegan's room to make the arranged meeting place six levels below the human section. They had been forced by Larson's goons to double back twice and at one point had climbed three levels up to go over a guard station.

Now Joyce was leading, light gripped in her teeth as she climbed down a narrow stone shaft. The ladder hadn't been used by anyone in years and the dust on the steps was making it slippery.

She could feel her fingers growing tender from all the climbing and scraping on the stone and she had long since lost the feeling in her feet from the cold. She had thought about stopping in her room to grab some heavier clothes, but then figured the risk just wasn't worth it. She'd go down into the cold again, but it wouldn't be that long until they were back up in the human levels fighting. She figured she could stand the cold for that long.

But now she was beginning to regret that decision.

She reached the seventh level down and stepped aside, waiting for Cray and Deegan to make their way down the shaft and join her. While she waited she flashed her light around the intersection of the vertical shaft and two horizontal shafts. She could go six directions from here into pitch-blackness and for some reason that made her feel safe. At least safe from the Professor's guards.

She glanced around at the dust on the floor, noting that a large number of men wearing boots had come this way at one point from the direction of the alien section. She flashed the light in the direction of where they were supposed to meet the others. No tracks at all in the dust. They would be making the first. That was both good and bad.

She let her light trail along the other tracks as Cray joined her and noticed what she was doing.

"Looks like a type of combat boot," Cray said, kneeling down and looking closely at one clear print.

"Larson's goons?" Joyce said.

Cray shook his head slowly. "I don't think so. They almost always wear a sneaker-type shoe that matches their green pants. Remember?"

Now that he mentioned it, she did. Sometimes they squeaked when they walked. She glanced down at the trail in the gray dust. "Then who?"

Cray shrugged. "Some of the Marines, maybe?"

"That can't be, unless they're old tracks."

"They don't look that old to me," Cray said and stood. "Of course, down here it might be hard to tell. They went down there." He pointed at the continuation of the shaft they had just climbed down. From her rough map it went down at least another four levels, maybe more.

"But the Marines are all dead," Joyce said, "Unless . . ."

"Dead?" both Deegan and Cray said almost simultaneously. Deegan jumped off the last step in the rock and joined them. "How can an entire platoon of Marines be dead?"

"I'm afraid it's very possible," Joyce said. "From what I heard the Professor promised to send them home, then landed their shuttle on the far side of the alien section."

"Maybe they fought their way free," Deegan said. "Marines are real good at that sort of thing."

"That they are," Joyce said. "When they have ammunition."

"And they didn't?" Deegan asked.

"That's right. They didn't." Her breath was making a swirling crystal pattern in the lamplight between them. "At least that's what Hank told me."

She glanced down the dark tunnel in the direction the tracks came from, then down the hole. What should they do? If it was the Marines, they would be a great help against the Professor. But if it wasn't, she could be walking into some sort of trap. And they were already late getting to the agreed meeting point.

She turned to Cray and Deegan. "I think we

need to get to the meeting, then maybe come back and follow those tracks."

Cray nodded. "Sounds logical."

"That it does, boss," Deegan said. "Lead the way."

With her rifle cradled in one arm and the light in the other, she headed off through the black tunnel at a quick pace. Her sneakers kicked up a fine spray of dust. This was the right decision. She knew it. But she was in a hurry to get back.

She tried to keep up a good pace to keep herself warm and she could hear Deegan panting behind her.

Three intersections later the tunnel made a sharp turn to the left and suddenly widened. A lantern held back some of the dark in the center of the large area and Joyce could see that three other tunnels came in from the left and two from the right like spokes off a lopsided hub. It was like the long room's walls had been decorated with rock and black holes. A very odd look the way the lantern was sitting in the center.

Crouched with their backs to the walls and rifles ready were Kent and two others, their guns trained on them.

"Hold your fire," Joyce said, quickly raising her hand and pointing her light into her own face so that they could see her. The three guns lowered and ten other men and two women with rifles stepped out of the black holes of nearby tunnels.

Kent smiled. "Glad you could make it."

"Two new recruits," Joyce said, and then quickly did the introductions for Cray and Deegan.

The others introduced themselves around the

circle and then Kent said, "Not all are back yet, I'm afraid."

"Hank? Jonathan?"

Kent shook his head. "I heard some shots up a few levels from where I was earlier, but I don't know who it was or what happened."

"Let's give them all some more time," Joyce said. She swallowed the thought that Hank might have been captured or killed. She wouldn't think about that. "With Larson's goons in some of the ventilation shafts, they might have had to circle a long way around to get here."

Kent nodded and pointed to three of the men who came out of the tunnels. "Might want to go back on guard duty."

They nodded and started to turn when Joyce said, "Hang on just a second. There might be something we need to do and I want everyone involved in the decision."

They all stopped, waiting for her, so she went on. "We saw a large number of tracks in the dust back about three hundred meters. It might be some of the Marines who survived being dumped into the alien sector."

"Really?" Kent asked, his voice clearly excited.

Another man said, "Would that be possible? Amazing."

Joyce glanced around and could tell they were all excited at the thought. There was no doubt the Marines would be on their side in the upcoming fight.

"The tracks looked like Marine boots," Cray said. "No telling how old the footprints are, but it should be pretty easy to track them to find out."

"Which," Joyce said, "if you all agree, is what I propose to do."

"God, yes," Kent said. He glanced around. "Anyone have objections in trying to find the Marines, if there are any of them still alive."

Seeing no objections, he turned back to Joyce. "What's your idea?"

Joyce pointed to Cray and Deegan. "The three of us head back and follow the tracks for an hour or so. If we have no luck we'll come back here within two hours."

"We'll wait," Kent said. He turned and pointed to a large crack in the stone abovehead high on one wall. "If we're not here, I'll leave you a note in that crack."

"Sounds good," Joyce said. "You two want to join me?" She turned to Cray and Deegan and both nodded.

"Anywhere you go, boss, I'm with you."

"There's no need, Captain Palmer." The voice was deep, solid, and seemed to fill in the room with a sound of command.

Everyone in the room dropped instantly to their stomachs on the floor in a wide circle, guns ready, pointing outward at the tunnels around them. Joyce could feel the sweat on her hands suddenly as she clicked the rifle to automatic fire and focused on the black hole in the wall. One leg was slightly draped over Cray's and it felt good there, like he would anchor her.

"We'll come to you," the voice said. "Don't fire."

Out of the shadows of the tunnel directly in front of Joyce stepped Sergeant Green, his hands in the air and a huge smile on his face. He had a bandage on his arm and was so covered with dirt and dust that he seemed gray.

A moment later, from every tunnel leading into the room, a Marine stepped forward into the light.

Joyce didn't know whether to shout for joy or be angry as hell that they had so easily been surrounded.

So instead she put her forehead down on the cold stone floor and said, under her breath, "Thank you. Thank you."

14

The Professor watched as Grace held her hand against the side of her head and seemed to listen into the distance. She kept shaking her head as if she didn't understand, but was close to catching whatever she was listening to. The Professor knew exactly what she was hearing. It was his rogue talking with the queen, probably challenging her. He knew the aliens communicated in some fashion, but he hadn't spent much time working on it. Now the secret had been handed to him, and that alone would make him famous.

"The signals still going on?" he asked without turning around. His feet were up on a computer console and his chair was tipped back, his hands behind his head. He felt as if the world were his for the taking. After so many failures, success had such a sweet taste.

"Yes, sir," Grace said, turning to him without taking her hand away from her ear. The signals seemed to be gaining in intensity and frequency.

The Professor jumped to his feet and strode up to the window. With a few quick key strokes he brought up the lights in the rogue's chamber to their highest intensity.

The room was a total disaster. The dismembered arms and legs, the torn and bitten bodies of the other ten male aliens, littered the room. Alien blood had been sprayed everywhere and now it ate into the walls and doors, leaving brown, smoking stains. The rogue's huge tail was thrashing back and forth, scattering body parts like so many leaves on a windy day. The crashes of the impacts sometimes shook the outer lab.

The Professor turned back to Joyce. "He's very agitated. Far more than I have ever seen him or any other male."

"It's stopped," Grace said suddenly. "It was very intense at the end on both sides, almost like two humans screaming at each other."

The Professor turned back to the window as the rogue moved suddenly. Now it seemed to have a very clear purpose. It toured the room once, quickly, crushing dead aliens' bodies and limbs under its feet.

Then it stopped in front of the window, studying the window and the room beyond for a moment. Then with a quick and very calculated move it twisted around hard, smashing its tail against

the window. A spiderweb of cracks spread out
from the point of impact.

"Grace! Look at that power, will you? A Marine
subsonic cannon at point-blank range couldn't
crack that glass. Amazing."

He turned to face her. "I think what you were
hearing must have been a challenge from the
queen."

She looked at him with a blank look and he realized he wasn't going to be able to share his joy
with her. She just wouldn't understand how important this was. She never could understand because she didn't have feelings. With a wave of his
hand he turned to watch his greatest creation in
its finest moment.

He stood a few meters in front of the glass, applauding, cheering, as the rogue's tail again hit the
window, sending a few splinters scattering around
the lab.

The glass was now a mass of webbed cracks.
The rogue tipped its head slightly, looking at it, then
charged straight forward at the Professor, its head
lowered like a bull.

Grace was android-quick. She caught the Professor in a full dive and they both tumbled out of
the way as the huge alien crashed through what
had been an unbreakable shield a few moments
before.

The Professor could feel Grace's hard, artificial
body twist to protect him as he fell, but he still
banged his elbow and knee hard on the tile, sending waves of pain through him.

With nothing more than a quick look at the Professor and Grace as they scrambled to their feet

behind a computer monitor, the rogue turned and headed for the alien sector.

Pausing only for a second, it ripped a hole in the block and stone wall between the lab and the corridor like it was so much tissue.

It stepped through the dust and rock, smashing blocks to sand under its weight. It stopped, slightly bent over under the lower ceiling of the corridor, then turned to the right and disappeared.

The Professor knew it was going for the queen.

Grace scrambled for the communications panel and hit two quick keys. "Red Alert! We have a bio-hazard breach in—"

"No!" the Professor yelled. "Cancel that order. Now!"

"But, Professor . . ."

Kleist looked at her directly and with his harshest voice said, "I don't want him so much as scratched. If he is, I will hold you responsible. Understand?"

He looked over at the hole in the wall where the rogue had gone. The dust was still settling from the air. His creation was so amazing, so wonderful, no one could harm it. No one would dare.

He turned back to squarely face Grace. "Now cancel that order and relay what I just said. I know where he's going and I want him in one piece when he gets there."

Then very calmly for a man who had almost been killed, he headed for his office. He knew where the rogue was going. He'd be there, in person, to watch the victory and cheer for his baby.

For almost two hours Hank had been curled up inside a small side ventilation duct.

He'd been heading for one of the small chemical labs to talk to his friend named Steve when he heard two of Larson's goons coming directly at him in the narrow ventilation tunnel. He'd ducked into the small side shaft that opened out through a screen knee high into one of the main corridors outside the labs.

Larson's two men had decided that this part of the ventilation system would be a good place to set up an ambush, so one had hidden in a side tunnel ten meters down and across the shaft from where Hank lay. The other had gone past Hank,

taking up a hidden spot five meters in the other
direction.

Hank couldn't come out of the narrow vent he
had crawled into fast enough to get a clear shot at
the one on the right, and if he even tried coming
out of the vent, the one on the left would hear
him and have a clear shot at his back. Hank would
be lucky to get to his knees before having his
body cut in half by a burst from a Kramer. It was
a prospect he didn't relish. So at least until the
changing of the guard, he was surrounded and
trapped.

For two hours he had lain on the cold stone of
the duct and waited, doing his best to move his
arms and legs slowly, to keep them as loose as
possible without making enough noise to attract
the guards. He ached in more places than he
thought possible, but every time he thought about
that he reminded himself he was still alive. That
thought always made the aches back off a little.

He had also managed to turn around so that he
was facing toward the grate covering the main
corridor and over the two hours he had silently
managed to take off all but one of the bolts holding the grate in place. If they did spot him he
could be through the grate and into the main corridor faster than they could crawl through the
small vent. At that point he'd be in the open, but
he'd take his chances there rather than a gunfight
with two men in a very narrow stone tunnel.

A huge crash from the direction of the lab
across the main corridor surprised Hank and he
banged his head against the stone ceiling. He
cursed under his breath, but didn't take his eyes

off the lab door. Three of Larson's guards came running down the corridor to Hank's right.

"What the hell was that?" one of the men said from the ventilation shaft behind Hank.

"It came from the Professor's private lab," the other said.

Hank was straining to see if the two men were coming his direction when right on top of him the world exploded. The entire wall of the lab across the corridor flew outward in a huge cloud of dust and flying rock, instantly crushing the three guards near it.

Hank covered his head just in time to keep from getting a face full of dust through the grate as one big rock bounced off the wall right above the opening of his vent. A few small pieces of rock dropped on him from the ceiling of the shaft, but luckily nothing big enough to pin him down.

Then, through the dust beyond the grate, Hank saw a nightmare appear.

His worst nightmare.

Any human's worst nightmare.

Ducking to fit into the ten-meter-tall corridor, a huge alien emerged from the hole in the wall of the lab and stopped directly in front of Hank's vent. The skeletal bones of its monstrous tail towered above him and Hank could barely make out through the dust the head and upper arms near the ceiling.

Aliens couldn't get that big, it wasn't possible. He'd read that somewhere.

Yet he was looking at one.

The alien swung its head to the right, then back to the left, as if getting its bearing. Then with steps that shook the stone around Hank, the alien went left.

Toward the alien section.

"Red Alert!" Hank heard Grace's voice over the base speaker systems. "We have a bio-hazard breach in . . ."

"Cancel that order!" Hank heard the Professor shout over Grace's voice. "I don't want him so much as scratched."

The public-address system clicked off.

"Holy shit!" one of the men in the ventilation system behind Hank said. "Let's get back."

The sound of their steps running off to the right was covered quickly by the distant sounds of the huge alien tearing at walls and doors as it fought its way through a human base built for beings one-tenth its size.

Down the corridor a few shots rang out and two people screamed.

"Damn good plan, guys," Hank said to the retreating guards as he quickly scooted away from the grate and the destruction beyond in the main corridor.

Even with his muscles stiff from lying on the cold stone for two hours, he started off at a run. At the first cross shaft he went down, taking the stone ladder as quickly as he could. He was very late for the meeting, but he hoped they had waited. This was news they would want to hear.

He hit the seventh level down and took off at a run toward the agreed meeting spot.

He didn't stop running until a Marine twenty meters from his destination stopped him cold in his tracks.

*   *   *

Joyce couldn't remember a sight making her so happy before. When those nineteen Marines came out of the shadows of the tunnels, she, for the first time since she was captured, let herself think about living through this and maybe getting back to Earth again to see her kids. She knew of Sergeant Green and knew how well trained the Marines were in fighting bugs. And since the Professor was a human bug that needed squashing, who better to do it?

She had climbed to her feet and greeted the Marines like the heroes they were, same as the rest of the rebels. After only a few seconds of cheering, Green had quickly pointed to three of his men and sent them back on guard duty down three of the five separate tunnels.

Then Green had asked for quiet and said, "We have a problem." He pointed after one of the guards. "Those three men are the only ones with live ammunition and that's because we ambushed three of Larson's men two levels down an hour ago. Anyone know where we might get some bullets?"

Joyce had been the first one to break the stunned silence with a hearty laugh. The others joined in and after a moment she moved up beside Sergeant Green and said, "It would be our pleasure to help."

Sergeant Green actually bowed in thanks and for doing that got a rounding cheer and applause from everyone.

She, Kent, Green, Robinsen, and Young all gathered against one wall. Joyce sat with her hands tucked in the bands of her pants hoping against hope to keep them warm as all their breaths froze into crystal cloud.

Other groups formed around the room with so many lanterns working that the high-ceiling stone corridor almost took on a comfortable feel.

They had just started talking about where to attack first and where to get more weapons and ammunition when, from the black mouth of one tunnel, Hank emerged, his hands in the air and a Marine right behind him.

Joyce felt her stomach ease another notch.

"Hank," she said as she rose from where she had been sitting and ran toward him. A few others, including Kent, surrounded him as she gave him a large hug that felt damn good. Then she stepped back and looked at him. His face was red and he seemed out of breath.

Green nodded to the Marine behind Hank who turned and disappeared back into the tunnel.

"You all right?" Joyce asked.

Hank nodded and moved over to the wall where he dropped down on the floor with his back against the stone. He took a few shuddering breaths, then looked up at Joyce and Sergeant Green.

"Just been running. And that Marine gave me a start, let me tell you. A good one, though." He laughed, then tried to take another few deep breaths.

Suddenly he seemed very serious. He looked first at Joyce who knelt beside him, then at Sergeant Green. "Did you hear the Red Alert a few minutes ago?"

"No," Joyce said.

"Red Alert?" Green asked, his voice almost choking.

Joyce glanced up at him. He had suddenly gone pale and he wasn't taking his eyes off of Hank.

"Red Alert, I'm afraid," Hank said. "A huge alien, obviously one of the Professor's experiments, broke down a wall from the lab and disappeared in the direction of the alien sector."

"Broke down a wall?" Green said. "How big was this bug?"

Hank shrugged. "Big. How tall is the corridor outside the main labs? Ten, maybe fifteen meters?"

Green nodded. "About that."

"The damn thing had to duck in there. Trust me, he tore a rock and concrete wall down like it was paper."

"Holy shit!" one of the Marines said behind Green.

Green kept staring directly at Hank. "And you say it was heading toward the alien sector? Did it seem like it knew what it was doing?"

"Now you have to understand, I was looking up at this thing through clouds of dust from a floor vent with two of Larson's goons in the shaft behind me, but I'd say it did."

Joyce turned to Green. "What does this mean? You've fought bugs before? Do they get that big?"

Green nodded. "Yeah, the queens do. But I can't imagine how the Professor had a queen trapped in his lab."

"It's a male," Hank said and again all eyes turned to him.

"Let's hope to God that's not possible," Green said.

"Well, when the Professor countermanded Grace's orders, I heard him say over the speakers that he didn't want *him* hurt. Clear as a bell."

"An alien's loose and he countermanded the orders? I don't—"

"It's a male all right," a voice said from behind the main group around Hank. Everyone turned and Joyce could see Cray, his face a pasty white in the lamplight. He seemed to be breathing fast and shallow and he was sweating even in the intense cold of the stone corridor.

"How do *you* know?" Green asked.

Cray took a deep, shuddering breath. "I was supposed to be its breakfast, but since the Professor had me strapped to a chair, it only looked me over. Real, real close." Clay opened his shirt and pointed to the huge red and scab-covered cut that ran across his chest. "It barely touched me with only one claw. It's as big as Hank was saying. Maybe bigger."

"And Kleist stopped the Red Alert?" Green shook his head. "That son of a bitch has totally lost it."

The silence in the tunnel echoed for a moment before Joyce turned to Green and asked, "Why did you want to know if it looked like it knew where it was heading?"

Green sighed. "Because if it really is that big, chances are the queen has called it. So the big male would head for the queen in the heart of the alien sector and it sure ain't going to use an airlock. Instead it's going to tear a hole all the way from the labs right into and through the side of the alien section. Those bugs are going to be everywhere in the human sector faster than Larson's goons can stop them."

Hank stood. "From the size of the hole in the lab, there won't be any plugging it ever. Actually, considering how long it took me to get down here, it's probably already open."

Green turned to Joyce. "I doubt the supplies we left in our old barracks are still there. We need weapons fast, the heavier the better."

"What about your guns?" Hank asked.

"Empty," Joyce said. "Except for the three on guard duty."

Hank glanced at Green, then unstrapped his rifle and ammunition belt and tossed it to Robinsen.

Green nodded to Robinsen and he took off at a quick pace down another tunnel to stand guard duty.

Joyce glanced at the rifle in her hands, then handed it to Green, who immediately tossed it to a private standing nearby and pointed to the other unguarded tunnel. "No heroics," he said.

"Now," Joyce said, facing Hank and Green. "We need a plan."

"And quick," Cray said, dropping down against the stone wall. "Trust me, you don't ever want to see that thing close-up."

Green laughed. "It's not the big male I'm worried about. It's the three hundred or so little ones that scare me."

Joyce shivered, and not just from the cold.

The screens on the Professor's wall showed the progress of the rogue as it tore its way toward the alien sector. The bodies of a blond-haired mother and her young daughter lay smashed against one wall on one screen, seemingly tossed aside like another small obstacle in the rogue's way.

The Professor watched for a moment, then, smiling and whistling, turned to finish putting on his armor. This was going to be the happiest day of his entire life. He had victory. His name would be listed with the great heroes of all time. He had solved the problems of the aliens.

Grace, already in her armor, scanned the station ahead of the rogue trying to warn people away with the address system. She was only partially successful.

The rogue was mostly through the human section and had now reached the corridor that ran along the extra thick barricade walls between the human and the alien sectors.

With a motion almost faster than the Professor could follow Grace focused every screen in the office on the areas up and down that hall and on the corridors and halls directly on the other side of the wall in the alien sector.

"They're massing, Professor," she said, pointing at the three screens that showed hundreds of alien males filling the corridors and walls and ceilings on the other side of the divide like a living coat of black paint.

"The queen sent them to defend her," he said, adjusting his microphone so it was against his mouth. Then he picked up the big Sound Cannon and cradled it under his arm. It felt good there, and he felt safer with it for some reason.

"I don't think so," Grace said. "They're not lining up in a defensive way. They seem to be mostly staying slightly back from the wall, out of the way, just waiting."

At that moment, on the human side, the rogue stopped, seeming to study a large airlock directly in front of it. Tilting its head from side to side it scanned the airlock. Then, in a mad and lightning-quick run, it darted forward, crashing headfirst into the airlock.

Stone shattered as the airlock was crushed outward, spinning down the corridor into the alien sector.

Thrashing like a wild beast the rogue proceeded to rip a huge hole in the rock and concrete barrier between the human sector and the alien side, sending up a huge storm of dust and rock.

In less than ten seconds the hole was a good twenty meters across and as high as the ceiling. A four-lane freeway could be built through that hole.

The Professor watched in total fascination as the massed aliens hesitated for a few moments, waiting for the rogue to get out of the way, then, as if on signal, they swarmed toward the new opening.

A few got in the way of the rogue and were crushed as it entered the alien section, acid blood splattering everywhere as if the rogue had stepped on a tomato. Without a glance back, it headed off into the depths toward the queen.

Ten of Larson's men were in the human corridor outside the breach as the aliens swarmed through, coming in on the floor, walls, and ceiling, faster than any human could follow. It was like ugly black water pouring from a huge spout. There was no stopping it.

A security-breach alarm screeched throughout

the station as the men fired at the aliens, then
broke ranks and tried to retreat. Most didn't make
it ten meters. The mass of aliens crushed them,
ripping the men's arms and legs off, biting through
their heads, smashing them flat like so much red
waste.

"Who initiated the security alarm?" the Professor demanded.

Grace just shrugged.

"I won't have my authority countermanded by
some gung-ho grunt! Put them all on report in that
area."

Grace just looked at him for a moment as he
stared at the monitors. Finally she said, "Professor, I must express my concern for your present
mental state."

"Excuse me?" he asked without looking at her.

"Your manner seems somewhat irrational, sir. I
am programmed to be concerned and to point
such matters out to you. Remember?"

Kleist turned to Grace, smiling. "My dear, no
matter how thoroughly you are programmed, you
will never remotely understand how I feel at this
moment."

He laughed and waved his arm at the monitors
where the black stream of aliens was still pouring
through the hole. "You think this is irrational?
This is nothing more than war." He faced her.
"What is important is that we shall soon witness
the validation of all I believe. In this godless universe there is man and the alien. Only one can be
the dominant species."

He turned back to the monitors and continued,
"Don't you understand what the rogue means?
No, I guess you don't, do you? Well, let me ex-

plain. You see, I have taken the brute clay of creation and reshaped it into a superior image. You must understand that point somewhat, being a creation of man yourself."

She said nothing so he went on.

"The rogue is our weapon. The alien empire will be destroyed at the hands of its own kind. The killing stroke? Bio-programming by human cunning and human intellect."

He raised his hands to the screens like they were an altar. "It begins here today."

Grace was silent for a moment, then she said in her normal voice, "We might want to proceed, sir."

He nodded, still staring at the monitors.

"We can go in from above," Grace said. "Considering the circumstances in the main areas, it might be a safer route."

He took his gaze off the monitors and the hundreds of aliens pouring into the human sector. The rogue was heading for the queen and she was sending her males at the same time against the humans who had imprisoned her. He laughed to himself. Never, ever underestimate the enemy, especially an alien queen.

But when his creation got through with her, there would be nothing left of this hive. Man may have a few casualties in this battle, but his creation was destined to win the war for humankind. And on that scale, what did a few meaningless lives matter?

He turned and headed for the door. "You're right, Grace. Quickly. I don't want to miss any of this. History is being made."

He smiled at her as she opened the hidden passageway and went through ahead of him.

16

Joyce glanced around at the group of very cold humans as Sergeant Green pulled the guards in from the tunnels and snapped a few orders. Nineteen Marines and twenty civilians with twenty-four rifles and two pistols among them. Not much of a force against over a hundred of Larson's goons plus the aliens. She was doubting that she would ever make it off this station alive. She just wished she could leave a message for her kids somewhere that it might be found. If she got the chance she would try to do just that.

In the quick meetings after Hank's arrival, they had decided that the best course of action was to get some real firepower, and the best way to do that was to break directly into Larson's armory. It

was located on the main human level, so it wasn't
going to be easy to get to, but it was possible.

They would have to assume that the alien sector had been opened and Larson's men were going
to have their hands full trying to stop the bugs, so
very few men would be on guard there. Actually,
both Clay and Kent argued that they should be
more worried about the aliens, but Green had
convinced them first things first.

Hank had insisted that Larson would never expect the Marines to be alive in the first place and
thus would think that the civilians would have no
reason to attack the armory, so no men at all
would be there. But Sergeant Green made a very
clear point that when it came to the Professor
and, to a lesser degree, Larson, they should never
be underestimated. He had done just that and had
ended up dumped in the far side of the alien sector.

Hank and Sergeant Green both knew the location of the armory, which turned out, much to
Joyce's relief, to be on the opposite side of the human sector from the alien hive. Kent knew how to
get them there through the lower-level tunnels and
straight up a mostly blocked vertical shaft. He'd
gone that way a few hours earlier and stumbled
on the shaft by accident when looking for a way
around a few of Larson's guards.

In the dust Kent drew them all a map to find
what he described as an old elevator shaft that
had totally been covered over when they built the
human sector and the labs. He said the ladders in
the shaft were mostly wood and fairly rotten, but
if used carefully, they would hold enough for them
to make the climb.

Sergeant Green made sure that Hank, Joyce, Cray, and his second in command, Robinsen, were all clear on the location of the opening of the abandoned elevator shaft, then assigned everyone into one of five groups with equal firepower and sent each off at top speed to meet as quickly as possible at the shaft.

Joyce found herself without a gun but in command of two Marines, Kent, and three other civilians. She was to take her group south for three tunnel intersections, a total of about two hundred meters. She was then to use that intersection's vertical shaft to go down three levels, then cross in a southeast direction under the human section to the elevator shaft.

Green's and the other two groups had just left leaving only hers and Hank's.

She reached out and gave Hank's hand a light squeeze.

"See you," he said, "in a few minutes."

She smiled. "Don't get lost." She wanted to say more, but didn't. She couldn't let worrying about him get in the way. It was like Danny and Jerry used to tell her during the war. If they made it, they made it. Worrying wasn't going to change a damned thing.

With one last quick smile at him, she turned and at a half run, with a light in her hand, led her group into her assigned tunnel. She stationed a blond-headed Marine named Private Rule to stay right near her with his rifle.

Another armed Marine named Warner she assigned to be last and guard their flank. Kent and the others were to stay in the middle and be damn quiet.

She was deep down tired from the day already, but the excitement of moving again with a real plan had the energy flowing through her system. She could barely hold her pace to a steady jog.

Being as silent as they could they made it through the first intersection and were approaching the second when the sound of shots echoed through the tunnels.

Joyce motioned for everyone to stop and they all listened. It seemed the shots had come from down at least a level and to the south. She turned to the Marine named Rule and pointed down at the vertical shaft in the intersection.

He nodded and she led the way to the shaft.

She was about to start down when Rule touched her shoulder and held up the gun. Then he indicated that he should go first and she agreed. With his rifle gripped in one hand, he quietly moved down the cut stone ladder. Joyce followed him closely until they reached the next level. No sign of any movement or even footprints in the dust, so she signaled for the others to join them.

More shots echoed through the tunnels as the last of her group were coming down. The shots seemed loud and very close. Joyce figured they were from one intersection over.

Another shot and a bullet bounced off stone and then scattered dust against a wall in a nearby tunnel.

She had everyone kill their lights and she let her eyes adjust in the pitch-black. Faintly, down the corridor to the right, she could see some sort of light.

She clicked her light on her own face, put her finger to her lips to indicate quiet, then pointed that Private Warner and one of the men should go down the right tunnel and swing around. She and Kent would go down the middle, directly at the light. The other two should circle around the other way led by Private Rule.

"Be careful you don't shoot one of our own," she whispered and they all nodded and silently split up.

Never had she felt so naked. Going into a firefight without a gun. That was stupid. A few steps into the tunnel she saw a rock the size of a grapefruit and picked it up. For some reason that made her feel better. A little stupid, but better.

Then a thought hit her that sent her blood rushing to her head. What would they do if the shots were being fired at aliens? What the hell was she going to do? Toss a rock at an alien? She forced the thought from her mind and focused ahead.

She clicked off her light again and with one hand resting lightly on Kent's arm moved toward the faint light around a shallow corner in the tunnel.

It seemed to take forever, but finally they had silently worked their way around the corner so they could at least see what was going on.

Ahead, crouched down behind a small pile of rocks from a shallow cave-in, were two of Larson's guards. They had their backs to Joyce and Kent and weren't firing at the moment, although both of their guns were poised on the rocks pointing down the tunnel in front of them. Their light had been tossed out in front of them and pointed where they were aiming.

Luckily for Joyce and Kent that at the moment no one was firing at the two. In this small space they were more likely to get hit by a ricochet from friendly fire than by shots from the two in front of them.

Joyce regripped the rock a few times, getting the feel of it in her hand. Then in the faint light she nodded to Kent who silently knelt and raised his rifle.

With as much force as she could she threw the rock overhand, imagining the two guys she aimed at were the two who had killed Jerry. She didn't realize she could throw that hard, or had that much anger inside her.

The rock seemed to take just a fraction of a second to cover the short distance. There wasn't even a slight arch in its trajectory as it flew, striking squarely into the back of the man closest to the wall. The thump was loud in the small tunnel as the rock bounced up and caught the guy a glancing blow in the back of the head. The force of the blow pitched him forward and face-first into the rocks in front of him. His head bounced and he turned blank-eyed to Joyce and Kent, blood streaming from his forehead as he slumped to a sitting position.

The other man, caught by surprise, took a moment to react to his bleeding partner, then he spun to fire.

Kent took him out with a single shot in the chest that sent him sprawling back over his buddy, blood spurting from his back like a pump-

ing fountain, staining the rocks and dusty floor a
dark black.

The single shot sounded huge in the small tunnel and Joyce covered her ears far, far too late.

"Sergeant? Hank?" Joyce shouted, her voice
sounding odd in her ringing ears. "Don't shoot."
She blinked her light twice in the signal they had
set up. "We got two of them here."

"Nice work," Sergeant Green said, a light ap-
pearing down the way. "I had my men working to
flank them too."

Joyce watched as the sergeant approached.

The guy she had hit wouldn't be moving for
some time to come. He wasn't dead, but he was
going to have one hell of a headache. She bent
over the guy she had knocked out and pulled his
rifle from his hands. She stripped him of his ammunition belt and slung it over her shoulder, then
emptied his pockets of six concussion grenades
and his flashlight.

The sergeant stood over the two for a moment
nodding. "Nice work. Two with one shot."

"A shot and a good right arm," Kent said. "She
should be pitching for the Yankees."

The sergeant, who was also unarmed, stripped
the other rifle from the bloody hands of the dead
man and checked to make sure it was ready to
fire. Then, without seeming to notice the blood at
all, took the guy's ammunition belt, grenades, and
light. Joyce smiled. Not only was the guy going to
wake up with a headache and a dead partner on
top of him, but in pitch-blackness and with no
light. A true hell. Served the guy right.

As Sergeant Green stood he slapped the stock
of the gun and smiled. "Feels much better."

Joyce had to agree. Having that gun in her hands did feel much better.

Much better indeed.

Sergeant Green's and Joyce's groups were the last to arrive at the old elevator shaft. Hank and Cray already had their groups climbing carefully up the old ladder and Sergeant Green went next, moving quickly and surely up the wooden ladder.

Joyce waited until there were only three Marines left before she strapped the rifle over her shoulder and started up.

The space was about four meters square and looked to have been some sort of freight elevator. Lights from the first people up had been left every ten meters, giving the place a weird glow.

At first she had imagined aliens swarming down the shaft at her, but again she forced the thought out of her mind. If that happened, she and all the others were dead. No point in thinking about it. But the chill remained with her for the next few minutes, even though her hands were already so cold she could barely feel them.

A dozen cables hung down the center of the elevator shaft and the wooden ladder was secured on old wooden beams up one side. Every few meters a horizontal beam gave the climber a larger step and Joyce took advantage of each of those beams. The wood of the ladder felt dry and very old, scraping her hands in the same places that they were already sore from climbing in the tunnels and vents.

At one point she had to stop and clear out a

splinter. But the entire way up, as Green had suggested, she kept her hands and feet away from the centers of the boards and never let her weight rest on only one spot at once.

She seemed to climb forever in the faint light, focusing only on her foot- and handholds, going slow to save what little energy she had left. Finally, when it seemed like the climb would become her lifetime hell, a friendly hand reached in from above and helped her through.

"You all right?" Hank whispered as he pulled her away from the elevator shaft and over against a wall so she'd have something to lean against while she caught her breath.

She took a quick glance around. No sign of Sergeant Green and Robinsen, but the rest seemed to be in a tunnel that had been blocked off when the human section was built.

"Tired, but alive," she said. "You?"

"About the same." His smile was like a shot of energy. She'd been lucky meeting this guy. Danny had been dead for years. Now Jerry was gone, too. If both of them got out of this alive, maybe it was time for her to get on with living and family. Maybe the kids could handle a new dad. Maybe they could get used to a mother around, once in a while, too. The way he looked at her, she had a sneaking hunch she might just be able to talk him into it.

She squeezed Hank's hand. Then nodding at the wall to the human sector, she asked, "What's happening?"

"Sarge and Kent are scouting the armory, seeing what kind of . . ."

Sarge ducked his head through a small open vent. "Let's move. Quick, through here."

Joyce slipped the rifle off her shoulder and followed Hank through the vent and into the well-lit and much warmer corridor. After spending so much time in the dark tunnels and ventilation shafts, standing again in the bright lights and carpeted corridor felt odd, exposed, almost naked. And very, very dirty. She immediately wanted to dust off her pants and vest, but refrained.

Green motioned that they should follow him and at a run they swarmed down the empty corridor to where Robinsen crouched behind a corner.

"Two of Larson's goons," he whispered. "Twenty meters. One standing on each side of the door to the armory. They look nervous, but I don't think they're worrying about us. They keep looking off toward the alien section to their right."

Green nodded and patted Robinsen on the shoulder. "You take the one on the right," he whispered. "I got the left. The rest of you be ready to run for the door when we do. There might be more inside, but we won't know that until we get there."

Robinsen nodded and clicked his rifle to single shot.

Joyce glanced down at hers, making sure it was set on fully automatic and the clip was full. She'd checked it three times already since taking it from the guard, but a fourth time never hurt.

Green and Robinsen were right beside the corner. "On two," Green whispered. "One."

"Two."

They both stepped calmly forward into the

corridor, swung, and took aim as if this were a practiced move and they were only shooting at ducks in a carnival booth.

They shot almost simultaneously, the concussion pounding Joyce's head and starting the ringing in her ears again.

Then both men started at a full run down the corridor toward the door of the armory as if the shots had been a starter's gun at a track meet. Joyce was around the corner two steps behind Green with Hank at her side. Behind her she could hear the pounding steps of the others.

Larson's two guards were clearly dead. One had been slammed against the wall with the force of the shot and had left a red smear down the stone face. The other had twisted sideways and lay in a heap in front of the door, a hole the size of a baseball blown through the back of his bloodstained jacket.

The door to the armory was locked but Robinsen made short work of it with a blast from his Kramer as two Marines scampered down the corridor toward the alien section to stand guard. Two others took up locations at the corner they had just come from. The more Joyce watched Green and his men work as a smoothly running machine, the more impressed she was. And damn glad to be on their side.

The armory was a large gymnasiumlike room with two armored tanks sitting in the very center. "Holy shit!" Green said after checking to make sure no guards were in the room.

Shelves and racks of guns, ammunition, grenades, and other such devices filled the walls and lined the center of the room around the tanks like

shelves in a library. Joyce knew what a lot of the
weapons were at first glance and had seen pictures of some of the others. But it was clear there
was enough firepower in this one room to stage a
pretty good-sized war.

"Everyone keep your eyes open for the Sound
Cannons," Green ordered. "We might need them
more than anything. Robinsen, take five men and
get as many ammunition belts as you can carry.
Run them back to the elevator shaft area."

Sergeant Green barked one quick order after
another.

Joyce stood to his right with Hank, marveling at
how organized the sergeant was and how quickly
he made decision after decision. Finally he turned
to them. "There's more ammunition over there.
You also might want to grab a few pistols and
stock your pockets with concussion grenades. As
many as you can comfortably carry without slowing you down. Speed may turn out to be your
most important weapon."

She nodded and as one she and Hank moved to
the shelves the sergeant indicated. She took two
more ammunition belts, their heavy weight a comfort over her shoulders. She already had six of the
small apple-sized grenades in her vest and pants
pockets, but she managed four more and a small
black pistol with a fifteen-round clip fit perfectly
down the back of her pants, held secure by her
belt.

Then, at a run and carrying three extra belts
each, she and Hank scrambled out of the door and
back down the hall toward the abandoned elevator shaft.

It seemed like the entire raid had taken forever,

but in reality from the first shot to ducking through the vent into the dark and cold of the tunnels, less than two minutes had expired.

Now they were armed. What next?

Find the Professor or the aliens?

Or just make a run for the ships.

So many ways to die, so few ways to live.

When the base was first being converted, the Professor had constructed three private tunnels known only to himself, Larson, and Grace. The three tunnels led from a hidden door in his inner office to the hangar deck, the center of the alien section, and the private lab. They were completely sealed and secure tunnels and at the moment the Professor was thanking himself for thinking ahead on this one thing.

He and Grace had ducked into the tunnels and had taken the right branch into the alien sector at a full jog, with Grace in front. Both were in full protective armor and Grace carried a Kramer, three belts of ammunition, and a motion detector. He put his trust in the Sound Cannon in his hand. Why kill an alien when you can just stop it in its tracks?

They reached the edge of the tunnel and Grace quickly scanned the area beyond the door with the motion detector. "Nothing," she said.

The Professor nodded and unsealed it, moving out onto a balcony that overlooked a huge room near the center of the alien sector.

"Still nothing," Grace said as they peered over the railing. The alien smell was intense, filling the Professor's nose and making it hard to breathe.

Under his boots he could feel the slime of the hive that had dripped off the ceiling and walls and ran across the floor.

"Nothing moving at all down here," Grace said. "No traces."

The Professor scanned the large room, then pointed at a large arch on the far wall. "Through there is the queen." He led the way to a stone ladder and they made their way down and across the room, moving as slowly and silently as they possibly could.

When they reached the archway he turned and glanced around again. "Fascinating. I at least expected there to be an inner cadre left behind to protect the queen."

"There was," Grace said. "This looks like what's left of them." She pointed through the arch toward the queen's inner chamber.

Thirty meters down the corridor were two bodies of large male aliens. The Professor moved quickly toward them. It looked as if they had been simply torn limb from limb. Their acid blood was dripping off the walls and pooling on the floor and he stepped carefully around it.

"I think you're right." He moved to study one body at close range. "See the different cranial configuration, the oversize mandibles? This was the queen's elite, her praetorian guard."

"Professor, over here. I have a trace."

Kleist spun away from the body. Grace was holding the sensor and facing down the corridor toward the queen's chamber.

"Is it the rogue?"

Grace shook her head in confusion. "I don't know. It might be. It's a large signal, but the form keeps shifting. I can't seem to get a lock on it. I can't explain it."

The Professor started toward the queen's chamber at a run, with Grace right behind him. He knew exactly what Grace was seeing, but he didn't want to take the time at the moment to explain it to her. Instead he would just show her.

The corridor suddenly widened into a huge chamber full of dripping slime formations and mounds of royal jelly, the new gold of mankind. The Professor halted just inside the queen's chamber, his gun lowered.

"Some things, Grace," he said, pointing, "need no explanation. Isn't this wonderful?"

Alien secretions had completely altered the shape of the room, creating a massive confusion of dripping forms from what had once been human balconies, railings, and ceilings. In clusters around the room were the ball-like egg sacks protected over by the queen and her guards. But now many of those sacks were destroyed, scattered or smashed in brown and gold stains.

Circling each other in the center of the room were the rogue and the queen. Both of an equal size, her maroon-colored skeletal frame and huge carapace contrasted with the metal black of the rogue. Massive amounts of saliva dripped from both their mouths and their second jaws extended and retracted like warning flags.

They circled each other, the queen somehow avoiding the egg sacks while the rogue smashed everything without notice. They weren't quite touching, but their front limbs were doing an intricate dance of position.

Suddenly Grace's hand went to the side of her

head. "They're screaming, Professor. Very intense, both of them."

"History is being made," Kleist said, and as if on cue, the rogue leapt, twisting its huge frame around the knocking the queen from her feet, biting hard on the back of the royal neck.

Grace held her weapon at the ready, but the Professor just watched, smiling.

He had no doubt who was going to win.

No doubt at all.

17

"**G**ather around," Sergeant Green said as the last of the men came through the grate. The narrow rock tunnel seemed almost warm with this many excited and sweating humans in it.

He waited until everyone was still, then said, "I figure we don't have much time until this entire base is overrun by the bugs. We got to round up every person we can, take care of some business, then get the hell out of here."

Joyce had never been so pleased to hear a sentence in her life. She wanted to applaud, and she could tell that many of the others around her felt the same.

"We're going to split up into three groups," the sergeant continued. "All with assignments."

He turned to face Joyce. "Captain, I want you to take all the civilians and make your way to the hangar deck. Get your ship and any other shuttle or transport parked there ready to fly."

He turned to the rest of the civilians. "How many of you can pilot a shuttle?"

Cray, Deegan, and Kent both indicated they could.

Green nodded, satisfied, then turned back to Joyce. "You and your people's job is to secure that hangar area and keep it secure for as long as you can. Understood?"

It was Joyce's turn to nod. She would have rather been going after the Professor and Larson, but she had a sneaking suspicion that special task was coming up for one of the Marine groups. In fact, she would bet just about anything that it would be Sergeant Green who would be taking care of it personally.

"If you can't hold the hangar area," Green continued, "get your asses into that ship and get the hell away from here. Don't wait for us, understand?"

Again she nodded.

"Good," the sergeant said. "The rest of us are going to be rounding up everyone we can and sending them your way. When you get a full ship, lift it. You all clear on that, also? Anyone have any questions?"

No one did, so he turned to Joyce. "Take as much ammunition as you can carry without slowing you down. And go slow."

She was about to start on the pile of ammunition belts when Sergeant Green said, "And one more thing."

He turned and looked at every civilian in the group. "Any of you fought bugs?"

Only Joyce and Cray nodded.

"A few basic words of advice. Aim for the head or knee joints. You hit one in the body and you'll spray acid blood in a ten- to fifteen-meter circle. They will come in above you more often than not and they move like lightning. Don't make a stand against them unless you have to. Hit and pull back, okay?"

He glanced around. "And pay attention to your nose. In an area like this you can smell the rotten bastards if they're nearby before you'll ever see them."

He hesitated, then looked right at Joyce. "One last thing. If a human is taken alive by an alien, they're better off dead than captured. Trust me on that one."

She knew that very clearly already. She'd seen more people, hung up alive in sacks with baby aliens growing inside them, than she ever wanted to remember. A person got like that and they were dead. The best thing another human could do was put them out of their misery real quick.

An uneasy silence filled the corridor. Finally Joyce said, "We'll be waiting for you on the hangar deck."

She hoped her voice sounded more confident than she felt.

Green nodded. "I know you will, Captain. That's why I gave you the job. Now get going. Me and the rest of the men here got some work to do."

Within thirty seconds Joyce had three belts of

ammunition over her shoulder, her Kramer cradled in her arms, and was leading nineteen other
civilians out the vent and to the right, down the
corridor, and away from the armory.

She only had one worry.

The hangar deck was on the other side of the
lab complex, and damn close to the alien section.

Too damn close.

Green watched the last of the civilians go
through the vent and down the corridor. Then he
faced his men, looking at Robinsen in particular.
He wished that Lynch were here, but Robinsen
was a good man. He'd do the job. He'd have to, or
not live to tell about it.

"Dillon. McPhillips. Young. Rule. And Bosewell.
You're with me." He looked at each man as he
called his name and each nodded. All five had
Kramers in their hands, four or five belts of ammunition wrapped around their chests, grenades,
pistols, knives, and God knows what else stuffed
into their pockets and belts.

He smiled slightly. If nothing else, they were going to make a mess of some things around this
good old base.

He turned to face his second in command. "The
rest of you are with Robinsen. Listen up, so he
doesn't have to repeat this."

Everyone took a step closer and Green went
on, talking directly to Robinsen. "I want you to
make a sweep through the living and recreational
areas of the base, rounding up and sending to the
hangar deck as many civilians as you can find."

"Will do, Sarge," Robinsen said.

"Use your best judgment on how to get the people to the ships. You might have to split up and send groups with guards, but I don't want any man striking out on his own. Stay in pairs. Is that understood?"

Again Robinsen, and every Marine behind him, nodded.

Green took a deep breath. "I figure we've got about an hour, maybe two if Captain Palmer and her crew can put up a good fight. So do the job and be back at the hangar deck in one hour. Kill any bug you see and terminate any human you see that's been taken by them."

Robinsen nodded. "Let's go, men. Hansen, take the point."

Green watched, satisfied, as Robinsen quickly had his twelve Marines through the vent and started to the left down the hall. Robinsen was the last through the vent and he hesitated for just a moment, glancing at Green. "See you in an hour," he said. "Then we're really heading home."

Green smiled. "You got it."

Robinsen smiled back. "Good hunting." Then he ducked through the vent and was gone.

Green took a deep breath and turned to face the five heavily armed men he had picked. "I guess you know what our mission is."

All five nodded and Green chuckled, smacking his Kramer to full automatic setting. "Then let's go get us some dog meat. Dillon, take the point and head right. Our first stop is Kleist's private office."

Green watched the men slap each other on the back, big smiles on their faces, and started for the vent opening with Dillon in the lead. The five Marines seemed excited, as if they had just hit the lottery and were going on the greatest trip ever.

Green dropped in behind Dillon. He had to admit, he was excited, too. It was payback time. The Professor and his damn bugs had been dishing it out to him and his men for three years.

Now it was their turn.

They were ready.

18

The corridors of Charon Base now felt very different to Joyce. Just a few days earlier she had walked this very hall with Hank, relaxed, arm-in-arm as they headed for her room. People had passed them, nodding hello, living their lives, going about their own business in what had seemed like a perfectly ordered world.

Now, less than two days later, she was again going down the same hall with Hank, only this time it was with eighteen other heavily armed people that she was in charge of. And they were all moving in single file, crouching, staying close to the walls, watching every grate and shadow carefully.

The hall was no longer a safe, warm place, and she was hoping like hell they could get out of it as fast as possible.

In the five minutes since they had left the Marines, they had heard some distant shooting, but otherwise there were no signs of people at all. The corridors had a deserted feel and she wondered where everyone was hiding.

They were approaching a major intersection, with a wide, carpeted hall leading off to her right and a smaller one branching to the left. If this had just been a regular day and she had been just ambling toward the flight deck to check on her ship, she would have gone right, walked about two hundred meters, then turned back to the right again after passing the long lab complex.

But today was different. She held up her hand for the column to stop and was relieved to see the two men at the end automatically set up to guard in the direction they had just come. They might not be as efficient as the Marines, but she believed they could take care of themselves just fine.

She turned to Hank and Kent and, keeping her voice low yet firm, asked, "Know of a good way from here?"

"Through the labs," Kent said. "By far the quickest and we don't spend much time out in the open."

"Didn't think you could get through that way," Hank said.

Kent gave a snort. "The Professor kept the door onto the flight deck shut off except for special deliveries or his own personal use. He made everyone else go around. His official reason was the decontamination chamber, of course."

"Through the labs, then," Joyce said. "Kent, you want to lead the way?"

He tapped his Kramer and smiled. "My pleasure." He quickly moved around her and with a quick look in both directions ducked around the corner and into the main hall.

Hank was right behind him and Joyce followed Hank. Behind her the rest stayed in line, almost matching them step for step.

The quick trip down the main corridor was uneventful as they stayed against the left wall and moved quickly in crouched positions as if they were running under low-hanging branches.

Kent pushed open a door labeled PRIVATE about a hundred paces down the hall. Carefully, gun at the ready, he checked in all directions, including above the door, and then went through indicating that they should follow.

They entered a large, airlock-style chamber, with places to hang clothes and supplies on both walls and a bench against the right. A window on the left opened into a small room where a guard would usually sit, but now was empty, the chair tipped over backward.

White lab coats were all that hung on the wall hooks now, with a few tossed carelessly on the bench like people were in a hurry to leave. Joyce wondered if that was a good sign, but she didn't say anything. If Kent thought this was the best and quickest way, she would let him lead. She had no better choices at the moment.

Kent did the same routine check beyond the inner door of the chamber and was through it just as fast. The white of the lab was almost blinding as she followed him down a white-tiled hall and around a corner into the main room. The shock of what she saw then brought her to a halt, her heart beating out of control in her chest.

This was the lab in the tape, the lab where Jerry's body had hung suspended in some sort of liquid until an alien had burst from his chest.

Twenty bodies still hung behind those huge windows, floating in a thick, clear liquid, tubes and wires holding them centered in place. Unlike in the tape, there were no lab techs watching the computers and monitors in front of the bodies. A few lights blinked, but otherwise the room was deserted except for the naked human bodies floating behind the glass.

"Jesus," Hank said, standing in front of one. "Isn't that Steven?"

The others gathered in front of the two huge walls in silence, as if they were standing in front of the gates of hell and looking in.

Joyce moved over and stood next to Hank, putting a hand gently on his shoulder. "A friend?" she asked.

He nodded. "Another controller, supposedly shipped home last month. He had a slightly deformed right hand which gave him a little trouble at times."

Hank pointed at the hand on the floating body in front of them. It had four natural-looking fingers, with another tiny, baby-looking finger in the position of the thumb. It would be a hard mark to miss. Obviously the Professor was getting to the point lately that he didn't care who knew he was lying about the bodies and how unlikely they were to be clones.

She glanced at the others. They had to get moving, yet they had to do something about this place. She couldn't leave it like this.

And she couldn't let those aliens inside those bodies hatch.

"Kent," she said, "which way out of here?"

He pointed to a white door near the far end of the left tank. "Leads through another bigger lab and then into the supply area. Beyond that is the hangar deck."

"Let's go, people," Joyce said.

One of the men down the line said, "We can't just leave them."

"We're not," Joyce said. She pulled a concussion grenade out of her pocket and tossed it a meter into the air so everyone could see. "About ten or so of these should do the trick, don't you think?"

Everyone cheered, and she motioned for Kent to lead the way into the next lab.

"Get everyone away from this area and save some room for me to come running. And watch your ass."

He nodded and waved for the people to follow him.

She held back Hank with a light touch. "Help me with this," she said. "Think you can throw five in quick succession?"

He had a grenade out of his pocket like a magician with a much-practiced trick. "Without a doubt."

"Sergeant Green told me these things have a

ten-second delay from pulling the pin to explosion. If we're both beside the door, you can toss five at the computers and monitors on the far wall. I'll toss five along the front of the glass and the monitors there. Ten of these babies should take out anything alive in this room."

"Without a doubt," Hank said. "Without a doubt."

They moved quickly over to the door as the last of the others went through.

Joyce stepped inside and quickly checked to make sure everyone was a safe distance away across the other white lab. Kent waved that they were ready.

"Let's do it," Joyce said, stepping back just inside the lab door and holding it open with her foot.

"On three.

"One."

"Two," Hank said.

"Three," they both said.

Joyce yanked the pin from the grenade in her hand and tossed it as hard as she could down the glass wall. She grabbed another grenade from her pocket, pulled the pin, and threw it.

One right after another, she pulled and threw. Paced, but as fast as she could.

Still, she was slightly slower than Hank, who managed a sixth right in front of the tank with his friend Steven in it just as she got her fifth away.

But she was through the door first.

She could feel his hand on her back shoving her forward at a dead run across the lab.

"The desk," Kent shouted. He pointed to an overturned desk he had fixed for a shield for them, then ducked behind a filing cabinet himself.

Joyce and Hank both went over the desk like two track stars and hit the slick tile floor on the other side sliding like two baseball players stealing second.

Then, on all fours they were scrambling back closer behind the desk when the first explosions ripped through the other lab. Dust and glass and splinters of wood exploded from the door they had come through seconds earlier like shot from the mouth of a cannon.

Joyce thought she could hear five, maybe six distinct explosions as the ground under them shook. Everything around them shook, some books and glassware crashed to the floor behind her.

She was about to stand when a very familiar odor hit her.

The smell of alien.

She spun around in time to see the black-shelled alien grab Cray from behind and pick him up like he weighed nothing at all.

Cray had been one of the farthest into the lab and had been taking cover behind a large tank near the far side of the room. The alien had come off the top of the tank from somewhere near the ceiling just as the explosion hit.

The instant Cray realized what had him, he twisted, using his right boot to kick out hard against the alien in a fruitless attempt to break free of its sharp claws. And for a second Joyce

thought he might make it. If he'd just been able to
drop free for a second the alien would have been
blown apart, but with it holding him, they didn't
dare fire.

Cray's struggles failed. The bug had him solid
with both hands, its claws cutting into Cray's arms
and stomach as Cray fought to free himself.

Suddenly it reared up, lifting Cray even farther
above the floor.

Before Joyce or anyone had time to react, the
bug's interior mandible shot out from its saliva-
dripping jaws, hitting Clay directly in the chest.

The back of Cray's shirt literally exploded,
showering bright red blood over the white tile like
a water balloon breaking on a sidewalk.

Kent, one of the closest to Cray, had his rifle
aimed on the bug trying to get a clear shot when
another alien dropped from behind him.

Three blasts from Kramers around Kent cut the
air, pulping the new bug against the wall behind
Kent and sending acid blood splattering in all directions.

Kent dove for cover under a desk and managed
to escape most of it, with a few drops burning
some holes in his pants and shoes.

It was clear to Joyce, however, that Cray was
dead. The alien's jaws had hit his heart and probably destroyed his spine.

"Take it out," she shouted.

Five Kramers spoke at once, sending the alien's
head and knees exploding like small bombs had
been planted in it.

As the alien's body did a slow twist for the
ground, still clutching the now obviously dead

Cray, Joyce shouted, "Watch your backs. Check the ceiling. Hank, cover me."

Everyone did as they were told as she took off toward the body of the alien and Cray. He looked dead, but she was going to make damn sure.

The alien's blood was eating ugly brown holes in the white tile and Cray was still held by the death grip of the claws. She got as close as she could, but there was no reaching him through all the acid.

Still, even from a five-meter distance she could tell he was dead. His blood had almost stopped pumping through the huge hole in his chest and back and his face had a look of terror glued on it. His eyes were wide open, staring off into his own personal hell.

"Joyce!" Hank screamed out. "Behind you!"

But his warning was too late. From the shadows below another tank, the alien rose up, grabbing her around the waist before she could even move. She could feel the cutting pinch of its claws as it lifted her and pulled her upward toward its mouth.

She twisted around, trying to bring the Kramer clutched in her hands to bear on its head, but the claws cut at her skin and she couldn't.

The only thought in her mind was, *I'm going to die.*

And I won't get to see my kids again.

The fight was going a little differently than the Professor had envisioned.

He and Grace had taken cover just inside a small archway leading into the queen's chamber as the rogue and the queen clawed at each other, their tails and feet smashing the bodies of her guards and the egg sacks around the floor. Golden royal jelly mixed with acid blood splashed the saliva-formed walls and twice the Professor and Grace's body armor had saved them from being burned by flying acid.

The rogue had seemed to have the upper hand at first and the Professor was sure his creation would soon defeat the queen. He had created something superior, far more powerful, far beyond the capabilities of anything nature could have created that he thought the fight would be over in seconds.

In the first contact the rogue had knocked the queen from her feet and had bitten through her lower shell, leaving an ugly wound. But instead of slowing her down the bite had enraged her even more and she had managed to push him off and regain her feet.

Now, except for a few swipes with their razor-sharp claws, they slowly circled each other, screaming at each other at a frequency that only Grace and other aliens could hear.

Ten full minutes now, and it still seemed to be a draw. But the Professor knew his creation would win.

Grace stood watching the battle, her feet spread, the Kramer in her hand always ready. The Professor sat on a stone near the tunnel opening into the chamber, never taking his eyes off the fight, the Sound Cannon beside him.

He was confident of the outcome. He had wagered everything he had, his entire life, on this fight. He knew he was right.

It was only a matter of time before the rogue proved it so.

19

The wall of monitors filled the office with pictures of horror beyond anything Sergeant Green had seen in his years of war. He had pushed Kleist's chair back out of the way and was standing behind the huge wooden desk staring at the screens.

McPhillips was working over the control board on the desk, switching pictures on the monitors as he quickly worked to figure the system out.

"Holy Christ," Dillon said as he too watched the monitors. "He could see every damn inch of this place."

"Makes you feel real clean, huh?" McPhillips said as he kept working.

Green was paying very little attention. His fo-

cus was on the screens and the terrible carnage
going on around the station. Bugs had totally
filled the area near the divide and Larson's men
looked like they had put up very little resistance.
A few bug bodies littered the huge hole in the barrier and a dozen bodies of Larson's goons lay scattered in the corridor on the human side, most of
them smashed or torn in half.

Now about thirty of Larson's men seemed to
have retreated into an area near the kitchens and
were holding off the bugs with pure firepower.
But Green knew they weren't going to last that
long in a pitched fight like that. The bugs always
seemed to have more bodies to throw at men than
men had ammunition to cut them down. Eventually the fight would turn to the bugs.

McPhillips glanced up at the screens focused
on the fight with Larson's men that Green was
watching. "Sarge, we aren't going to their rescue,
are we?"

Green glanced over at McPhillips and laughed.
"Are you kidding? See if you can locate Robinsen
and his men."

McPhillips smiled and went back to work on
the control panel. On the huge wall of monitors
scenes changed with only a flickering. One moment a monitor was filled with the terrorized
faces of a man and a woman huddled in a closet
in a small bedroom. The next was a scene of an
alien carrying a passed-out lab tech in a white
coat toward the alien section.

The west lounge kept flashing up from different
cameras as McPhillips worked. A large black male
alien was making a home behind the bar, spread-
ing saliva over the bottles, coating everything

from the bar stools to the plants with the slime he excreted. Draped over the corner booth was a tall black man with his head cut off.

Another monitor flickered, another scene.

A man fired at two aliens, blowing one apart, but missing the second. The guy's blood exploded over the camera as the alien ripped off his leg and bit through his chest.

"Jesus," Dillon said. "They're everywhere."

Green glanced around at Dillon, whose face was as white as he had ever seen it. The kid's eyes were huge and he seemed to be staring at the monitors. He was going to be no good if he didn't move soon.

"Dillon," Green said, his voice sharp enough to get through. "Relieve Bosewell on guard."

With another quick glance at the wall of monitors, Dillon nodded and left the room.

Green glanced back up at the wall and all the pictures that were making him as sick as Dillon looked. It was clear from this that he may have sent Robinsen and the rest of the men into a suicide mission. He just hoped Robinsen had enough sense to know when to retreat.

A scene of a young woman hiding alone with a pistol in her bathtub. Green hoped she had enough sense to use it on herself before any alien found her.

Another monitor flickered and Green found his attention drawn to two women armed with Kramers ducking down a side hall going in the direction of the hangar deck. They looked like they might make it, if they were lucky. Maybe Robinsen had sent them.

Another monitor flickered and Larson appeared, working frantically on a Sound Cannon.

"Hold it!" Green shouted to McPhillips and then pointed to the monitor showing Larson bent over the counter working. "Can you spot where he's at?"

"Just a sec." McPhillips studied the board, then glanced up at the monitor showing Larson. Then he laughed. "The son of a bitch is in a small private lab just behind this office. I doubt he even knows we're here."

"Is he alone in there?"

"We'd see anyone if there was. It's a small place. See what's in those tanks around him?"

Green looked beyond where Larson was working at the glass tanks on the shelves above him. It took him a moment, but then he realized what he was looking at. Tanks full of live face-huggers, stored right beside his office. The Professor was crazier than they thought.

"How do I get there?" Green asked, checking to make sure there was a full clip in his Kramer.

McPhillips studied the board for a moment, then a center screen flashed up a map. Both of them studied it, then McPhillips pointed to a metal door near the small kitchen in the back of the huge office. "Right through there."

Bosewell came through the big doors. "Rule and Dillon on guard." He glanced up and saw the wall of monitors and stopped cold. "Holy shit," he whispered under his breath.

"You want to watch some fun?" Green said. "Keep your eye on that third monitor from the top near the right corner." He pointed at the wall, then strode toward the door near the kitchen. He'd been wanting to do this for years and now it was finally here. His hands were shaking he was so excited.

"Sarge," McPhillips said from behind him as he reached the door. "You need backup?"

Green turned and smiled. "Nope. This guy is all mine. But you can watch the fun."

Green pulled the Kramer back under his arm and drew a small pistol out of his belt. He made sure the ten-shot clip was full. It was his favorite pistol and he was damn accurate with it. Unlike the Kramer, it would slow Larson down, but it wouldn't kill him.

And for what he had in mind for Larson, that was a good thing.

He took a deep breath and then looked back across the room at the monitor. Larson was bent over intently studying the works of the Sound Cannon.

McPhillips gave him a thumbs-up.

Green silently clicked the latch on the door, then yanked it open so hard it splintered some wood off the wall behind it.

With a quick step he was through and into the small storage area facing Larson's back.

Obviously startled, Larson reached for his Kramer lying beside him on the counter.

"Don't even think about it," Green said and Larson stopped, frozen.

"Face me with your hands up," Green said and Larson did as he was told, moving his hands away from the Kramer.

When he saw Green, he smiled. "So the Professor was right. You weren't dead."

"Too bad for you," Green said. He stared into the dark, black eyes of the man he had hated for so long. This man had killed so many of his men he had to be made to suffer. Killing him was just too easy.

"You're going to need the cannon," Larson said, pointing to the one he was working on. "Besides the one the Professor has, it's the only other big one on the base and it's broken from your last mission. Remember?"

Green didn't say a word and didn't change his expression. He would just let Larson talk for a moment.

"I think I can fix it," Larson said. "Just give me a little time and a promise to take me with you when I'm done."

Green smiled. "Trying to make a deal?"

Sweat was pouring off Larson's white forehead and his eyes were starting to glance back and forth, looking for any way out.

"Just trying to not get killed by you or the damn bugs."

"Oh," Green said softly. "I won't kill you."

The look on Larson's face was starting to lighten, as if he actually believed what Green had said.

Green lowered the aim of his pistol from Larson's chest to his right leg and shot.

Larson's scream echoed in the small room as he grabbed the hole in his upper thigh and fell to the ground. Blood flowed quickly into a small pool on the tile floor.

With another carefully aimed shot Green hit Larson in the other leg.

Larson screamed again.

"Hurts a bit?" Green said, smiling at Larson.

The sergeant moved around the man twisting on the floor and grabbed both his Kramer and the broken Sound Cannon. Holding them under one arm and keeping the pistol aimed at Larson, he moved back to the door and checked to make sure it would still latch solid. It would.

"Don't—don't kill me," Larson said, holding his bleeding legs and looking up at Green.

Again Green laughed. "You don't listen real well, do you. I said I wouldn't kill you."

"Then why'd you do this?"

Green shrugged. "I suppose because I've wanted to for years."

Larson looked at him, the hate boiling away the pain in the man's eyes.

Green stood in the open door staring down at the man he had hated only second to the Professor. At this moment, finally seeing Larson get his reward, he felt wonderful, like he was a kid again getting his first kiss. There was a twisting, excited feel in his stomach.

"You can't leave me like this," Larson said. "I won't stand a chance."

Green nodded. "I suppose that's true. All right. I won't leave you like this if you tell me where the Professor is."

Larson shook his head. "I don't know where he's at. He and that damned android of his got all suited up and disappeared. They were following that huge bug of his into the alien sector. I imagine he's dead by now."

"Now, now," Green said, pointing the gun at him again. "You wouldn't lie to me, would you?"

Larson, sweat pouring off his face, shook his head back and forth. "It's God's truth. He followed that damn monster of his. He was as crazy as a loony bird, I swear."

"Now that's the truth," Green said. "Thanks."

"I was just following his orders," Larson said, his eyes begging Green. "He killed all your men. Not me. I'll even help you find him if you want."

"You'd have a tough time walking, I'm afraid," Green said. He made a motion to close the door.

"Wait!" Larson screamed. "I thought we had a deal."

Green sighed. "I guess you're right. I did promise that if you told me where the Professor was, I wouldn't leave you like this."

Larson nodded, his eyes begging.

"And I suppose you did tell me the Professor's location, so you held up your end of the bargain."

"That's right. I did."

Green looked around at the tanks and then smiled. "Then I think it's only fair that I give you the same chance you gave my men."

With three quick shots he broke the glass on three of the face-hugger tanks, sending clear fluid cascading down over counters and onto the floor where it mixed into a pink swirling river with Larson's blood.

Green saw one of the face-huggers slip off the counter and start for Larson as he shut the door tight and locked it.

Beyond the door he heard Larson shout, "Oh, God! Noooooo!"

Green smiled as he turned back to his men who were both applauding like crazy.

He took a deep bow.

Then he looked at them and let the biggest smile he had ever remembered feeling cross his face. "God, that was fun!"

20

The alien's sharp claws were cutting at her chest and arms as it raised her from the floor like a child and held her in front of its ugly face.

This had to be a nightmare. This couldn't be real. She would wake up screaming at any moment. She wasn't about to die after all this time in the same way Danny had died.

This had been her nightmare more nights than she had ever wanted to count and now it was coming true.

God damn it all to hell! She wanted to see her children just one more time.

But that wasn't going to be possible.

She was going to die.

The teeth of the alien seemed only inches from her face. Saliva dripped from them as it slowly opened its mouth. She twisted back and forth, doing everything in her power to pull the Kramer up and aim it anywhere near that ugly mouth and head. But the claws only cut her arms and stomach deeper the more she struggled.

Inside, down in the black hole of its mouth, she could see the second set of teeth gleaming, pulsing like they wanted to come pouring out and ram through her face.

"Hold still!" Hank's voice screamed behind her. Somehow, through her sheer terror, through the silent screams she was afraid to let go of, she heard him. Hold still. Shit, what choice did she have? She could do that. She didn't want to. She wanted to scream and twist and get free and run like hell. But somewhere deep inside she understood Hank's command.

She froze, forcing her body to become as rigid as possible, her eyes focused on the wide-open jaws of the alien.

Her willpower stopped her from throwing up her last energy snack. Her eyes watered from the pain and the thick smell of alien rot as she forced them to stay totally open.

Behind her she heard Hank shout, "The glass behind her! Blow it out!"

Almost instantly the roaring sound of a half-dozen Kramers on fully automatic filled the room, mixing with the sound of glass shattering and water pouring like a river gone wild.

Her mind screamed, *What the hell was he doing?*

But she kept her body frozen like a log.

The alien glanced away from her.

Then suddenly everything went crazy at once.

It felt as if someone had pulled the rug out from under her captor. The bug jerked her up, then sharply down, the claws digging even harder into her flesh as the wall of water from behind the broken glass hit its legs.

And then it let go of her as it went over backward.

She slammed hard into the floor. The impact knocked the wind out of her and the water sent her tumbling across the hard tiles. She felt wrapped in a thick, oily jell. Slime.

She did her best to tuck and roll, but she still banged her head twice, both times hard, before she finally stopped sliding.

Again the sounds of Kramers screaming filled her every sense. Through her spinning head she had just enough thought to hope she was far enough away from that bug they were toasting to keep out of the acid. She covered her head and face and waited for the deadly shower.

It didn't come.

Hank shouted, "Form a circle and watch every shadow and corner." Then after what seemed like a long time but actually was only a moment, he was at her side, rolling her gently over on the wet floor.

She opened her eyes, letting the room spin for a moment around her like she'd had way too much to drink.

"You all right?" Hank asked, and she could see the look of panic and concern on both his and Kent's face spinning over her.

She took a deep breath and exhaled. The room slowed its spinning and almost stayed put.

Almost.

She took another deep breath and it stopped. Thank God.

She reached up and touched Hank's face gently. "Did you get the number of that damn truck that hit me?"

Hank looked at her for a moment, then laughed deep in his throat.

God she loved that laugh of his.

And this one special laugh was one she was going to remember for a long, long time.

Assuming, of course, she lived through the next hour.

"I think I found them," McPhillips said as he punched up one monitor and then another, filling the center of the wall with pictures from different angles of a main corridor in the living quarters.

"Oh, God, no!" Bosewell said.

Green felt his stomach twist with his worst fear. The joy he had felt from killing Larson a minute before was now totally gone, drained by the scene he saw on the wall.

Three of his Marines lay dead in the middle of the wide main corridor. Teppo had his head cut off and one arm was missing. Freeman was soaked in acid, his skin boiled away, his face missing. Bond had been gored through the chest by an alien jaw, his legs ripped from his body. All three still held their Kramers and looked as if they had all gone down fighting to the end.

Seven, maybe eight alien bodies were scattered

down the hall, attesting to the fight the men had put up.

"Scan down the hall farther," Green ordered. God, please, don't let it be all of them.

"Which way?"

"Into the living sector."

McPhillips did as he was told and each new monitor showed more horror. A hundred meters up from the three dead Marines was a group of fifteen civilian bodies. Six dead aliens lay around them, most with their heads shot off, some with their legs gone.

But what had killed the civilians had been acid from the body of an alien beside them.

From the way it looked a bug was bearing down on them and one of the civilians had just opened fire at the alien's body, causing the acid blood to pour over the humans in a flood of death.

All their clothes had melted away and the entire mess was a steaming, ugly pile of red meat, human skeletons, skulls, and brown acid blood.

Behind him Green heard Bosewell throwing up. He didn't blame the man. He felt like doing the same thing.

He took a deep breath. "Keep scanning," he told McPhillips, who after a moment did as he was told.

After what seemed like a long few minutes of finding nothing in either direction, McPhillips turned to Green. "Looks like that was just one firefight."

Green nodded. It looked that way to him, also. Robinsen must have assigned the three men to try to get the group of civilians back to the hangar deck and they'd been ambushed in the corridor.

"Can you find the rest of the men?"

McPhillips shrugged. "I could if I had a few hours and if they haven't ducked into the ventilation tunnels and gone down."

Green nodded. It did look hopeless. He was just going to have to hope Robinsen and the rest of the men could fight their way to the ship. But now it might not be a bad idea to get there themselves. If the Professor was in the center of the alien section, they sure as hell weren't going in after him. He was as good as dead and Green's only wish was that he die slowly, with a face-hugger tight on his face.

"Can you find the hangar deck quickly?"

"Not a problem," McPhillips said and within a few seconds had four different views of the deck on the monitors.

"Nothing but bugs," McPhillips said softly, expressing the obvious.

Two aliens were on top of Captain Palmer's shuttle and a good dozen more were scattered around in plain sight. God only knew how many were in hiding in those shadows and storage bays.

Palmer and the rest of them were walking into a huge nightmare.

"Let's move!" Green shouted and headed for the door at a full run.

"Hang on a minute!" McPhillips shouted. Green turned around. "Sarge, I think there's a better way."

"Make it quick."

McPhillips's fingers danced over the control board and again the map of the surrounding area filled the middle screen. "The Professor's got some private tunnels from here." He pointed at the bookcase behind him. "I spotted them on the map when we were looking for Larson's location. One dumps directly onto the flight deck."

Green nodded. "Good work. Now let's find it."

Thirty seconds later they had the hidden door open and with Green on point and Rule bringing up the rear they were at a full trot for the hangar deck.

Green just hoped they would be in time to help.

21

No more aliens appeared in the ten minutes it took for Kent to get Joyce's wounds bandaged and for her head to stop spinning. She still felt light-headed when she stood and the lump just above her hairline hurt like hell, but otherwise she was going to live.

The room looked like a hurricane had hit it. All the floors were covered with an inch-deep, jelly-thick water that made the footing slippery at best, and the place smelled a combination of alien rot and her son's chemistry set.

She was wet, bruised, and cut, but alive. That just amazed her. Every time she even blinked she saw the razor teeth of that alien inches from her face and the second mandible waiting to cut through her. But when she kept her eyes open, she knew she was alive.

She gave Hank's hand a final squeeze to say thank you one more time and let him know she was all right. He'd stayed with her like a worried mother, hovering over her while Kent had mended the cuts from the alien's claws. He'd saved her life, and now she was even more determined to get them both off this rock and back home safely.

She did a quick check of her Kramer to make sure it was all in working order, then glanced around at the men circled in defensive positions around her. Five, maybe six dead aliens littered the white lab around them and Cray's body had washed against one of them in a grotesque loverlike position. Behind his body, the wall of glass they had broken to knock out the alien holding her had a human body hanging in it by the wires over his face. Another one of the Professor's experiments. Looking at that body there, she really hoped Green was having some luck finding the Professor and Larson. They deserved whatever Green could give them, and much, much more.

"Everyone ready to see if we can make it to the ship?" she called out, her voice echoing through the big lab and over the dead bodies of the aliens and Cray.

Nods and a few "anytimes" answered her question.

She took a deep breath. "Kent, lead the way. Stay close, people. If the bugs were in here, they for damn sure are going to be on the hangar deck."

Kent patted her shoulder as he passed her and headed for a double-sized brown door on the far side of the lab. Three others dropped in beside him and then she and Hank dropped into line behind them.

She didn't even look at Cray's body as they passed. That could have well been her there beside him. She didn't want to think anymore about that than she already was. Instead she looked at every shadow, at every corner as if an alien was going to come around it at any moment.

From the jerky movements of everyone else's heads, they were all doing the same. They were scared to death, and they all had a right to be.

Kent reached the wide double doors that had obviously been designed to move large equipment from the hangar and storage areas into the labs.

"Hang on until we get into position," Joyce said.

Six of them, including her and Hank, knelt or stood in firing positions facing the door. The others backed off, guns up and ready for anything.

She glanced around to make sure everyone was in position, then said, "Go!"

Kent threw open both doors and jumped back out of the way.

Beyond was a fifty-meter-long room with high shelves on both sides and another double door on the far end. It was brightly lit and clean. Assortments of laboratory equipment and supplies filled the shelves and two carts were parked near the center.

She studied the room slowly and carefully. Nothing seemed to be moving and she could see no sign of alien slime on any of the shelves or the clean white floor.

"Four down one side," Joyce said, "and four others down the other. Stay close to the shelves and protect each other's back. Set up a defensive position at the other doors without opening them. The rest guard our rear and cover them from here."

Kent motioned for three men to follow down the left side of the storage room and Hank on the other side did the same. Joyce positioned herself square in the middle of the door with five others around her and they covered the eight men every inch of the way to the other side.

"No signs at all," Kent shouted as he reached the other door.

"Yeah, looks clean in here," Hank shouted.

"Cover us," Joyce shouted back and Hank nodded.

She turned to the men guarding the room behind her. "Fall back inside the storage room and let's get these doors closed. Better than being out here in the open."

They did as they were told and within a few seconds the big double doors were closed behind them. It wouldn't hold an alien out, but if one came crashing through at least they'd have some warning.

"Four of you stay here and keep the rest of us covered." She turned and started right down the middle of the room toward Hank and Kent. After all this, if she couldn't trust their judgment now, who could she trust.

As she strode through the supply room, her gaze scanning the high shelves, she caught sight of a ventilation grate above the top shelf on the right. There was another directly across from it on the left. She stopped and picked out two men. "Keep a gun aimed at those vents," she said, pointing at the grates. "And if your arms get tired, get someone to take your place. They'll come in that way, if at all."

Two men did as she said and she joined Hank and Kent who had come back to the middle of the room to meet her.

"We got a reprieve, but a short one," she said. "Somehow we have to get to the ship. Off this rock is the only safe place."

Deegan, who had been staying near the back of the group in the other lab, moved up beside her. "Boss," he said, "from what I can figure, the ship is about fifty, maybe sixty meters straight off these doors."

"Can you remember anything of what's between here and there?" Kent asked.

"Just open deck," Deegan said. "A lot of it. Normally there'd be another shuttle there, but I heard the Marines took off in that one."

"Yeah," Kent said. "A direct flight to the alien section."

"Suggestions?" she asked. She didn't have any bright ideas at the moment herself. Covering fifty meters of open deck while fighting off aliens was going to be an ugly task at best. And probably fatal.

On top of that it would take a good thirty seconds to cycle the airlock on the ship if it was closed. If it was open they were going to have to clean the ship of bugs. She hoped like hell it was closed and sealed like it was supposed to be when no one was on board.

"Form a circle and run for it?" Deegan suggested, but both Kent and Hank shook their heads no.

"Won't work," Hank said. "They'll rush us so fast that we'll cover ourselves in acid when we cut them down. I've seen it happen before."

Kent nodded. "I agree. We're better off going in small groups, enough to cover each other and fight our way slowly from different directions toward the ship."

Joyce nodded. She had a clear memory of a group of kids and two adults being covered by acid back on Earth when one of the adults had shot an onrushing alien in the body at close range. The momentum of the bug had carried it and its acid blood over all the kids. Thank God none of them had lived.

Joyce glanced around the long storage room at the eighteen men, most of whom had their weapons at the ready as they continually scanned the room. Nineteen of them total. That made a good round number.

She turned back to Hank and Kent and Deegan. "I agree with Kent," she said. "Three groups of four and one of seven up the middle. Each group moves slow and not only covers themselves on all sides, but tries to cover the others as well."

Hank turned to Kent and Deegan. "Kent, you got a better memory than I do for these things.

How wide is the room to the left and right of here?"

Kent pointed to his right as he faced the hangar doors. "Main passageway and decontamination area is that way about twenty meters along that wall. Beyond it is maintenance another twenty meters. There's a balcony over the decontamination area. It's a square room in that direction, but I wouldn't suggest we get too close to the main entrance."

"I agree," Joyce said.

"In the other direction," Kent said, "is mostly just blank walls of rock. I suppose they left it unfinished in that direction in case they needed to expand the hangar deck. Not much chance of that now."

"So fewer places for bugs to hide on the left of the doors."

"A lot fewer," Kent said.

"And a better angle at the ship," Deegan said. "Coming at it from the nose will allow us to see both sides and not get surprised by a bug coming over or under the ship."

Joyce patted him hard on the back. "I always knew there were brains in there," she said, smiling.

"Damn, blew my cover," Deegan said.

Joyce turned to Kent. "Take three men and be ready to go first out the door and duck left. We'll cover you from the door. Stop with your backs to the wall after about fifteen meters and cover us."

Next she turned to Deegan. "You pick three men and be ready to go out ten seconds after Kent. Go even farther left along the wall and again set up a defensive position so that you can see the ship and the deck between here and there."

Deegan nodded.

"Someone needs to guard the right," Hank said. "I can take three men and just go a few meters to defend from there."

Joyce nodded. "I'll lead the rest strung out toward the ship across the deck. When you three feel the time is right, start your men toward the ship, too. Don't wait too long because we don't want to get too spread out. Ideally we should all be closing in on the ship about the same time.

"And, Deegan, like you said, get far enough around to the left so you can see the far side of the ship and keep it clear as you come in."

"No problem, boss."

She glanced around, then took a deep breath. "Well, the longer we wait, the more bugs there'll be to kill."

Kent turned and motioned to the three men who were nearest the hangar doors that they were with him. Hank and Deegan did the same and she told the rest in the room to follow her slowly across the deck when she started out.

Then, with six Kramers pointed directly at the wide double doors to the hangar deck, she nodded for Kent to open them quickly. And very wide.

What she saw made her sick. Aliens. Everywhere.

A fraction of a second later six automatic rifles were firing fast and hard, with others around them joining in.

Kent had opened the doors into hell.

So much for careful planning.

The battle was going poorly as far as the Professor was concerned.

The two huge aliens circled each other, saliva dripping off their teeth like open faucets, their arms waving and slashing, usually missing. Both tails swished back and forth, sometimes hard and fast, sometimes slow and mean.

The huge queen's chamber was a wreck from their dance of destruction. Alien formations had been cut to the ground, pulling the human constructions like balconies and ladders under them down with them. Golden royal jelly, masses of it, a multiple fortune on the black market back on Earth, had been splattered and mixed with acid blood and saliva.

In thirty minutes of circling and fighting, the queen was slowly gaining the upper hand over the rogue.

At first it looked as if he would win easily and the Professor had been so excited. But as he and Grace watched, the advantage shifted to the queen.

She was the crafty one.

She was the smart one.

She had avoided the rogue's lunges after the first one and had slashed him again and again with her sharp tail and claws, letting his acid blood flow down his legs. Everywhere he stepped now he left bloody prints.

Compared to her, he was a clumsy oaf, smashing everything, wasting energy as she dodged away from his frantic attacks more quickly with each passing minute.

"This shouldn't be happening," the Professor growled. "He's bigger and stronger than her. He's a killing machine. She should be dead by now."

Grace hadn't answered any of his ramblings for the past twenty minutes. She stood just inside the small side tunnel they had taken refuge in, Kramer in hand, keeping a sharp eye not only on the two huge aliens in front of them, but on the black tunnel behind them. So far no alien had dared get near this area, but she was taking no chances.

The Professor moved forward and now stood just on the edge of the royal chamber, his helmet off, the Sound Cannon clutched almost unnoticed in his right hand.

Grace's hand went to the side of her head suddenly, as if she was almost in pain. "Sir, they're screaming at each other again."

"It's about to end," he said. "Now he will win. You just watch."

But just as he spoke the queen lunged for the first time in the battle.

She caught the rogue in the side and her tail whipped around and cut off the rogue's left arm as they tumbled to the ground and rolled hard enough to shake the stone under the Professor's feet.

"No!" the Professor shouted, taking a few more steps into the chamber. But his scream was lost and small against the sounds of the titan battle going on in front of him.

Grace stayed beside him, protecting him.

But the queen didn't notice them. She had the rogue gripped by the neck now in her giant teeth, and was twisting, doing her best to bite off a huge chunk of the rogue's plates and skeleton.

The rogue was on his side, thrashing, alien blood spurting from the stump of his arm.

The queen's razor-sharp tail again spun in the air, flicking back and forth before slicing into the rogue's side with an ugly, thick smacking sound.

Alien blood sprayed over the nearby wall and a few drops splattered near the Professor, but he didn't notice. His creation was being killed. He didn't believe it, even though he was seeing it.

He had been wrong again.

"The screams have changed," Grace said. "Now it's only one and it sounds more like pain than a challenge."

The queen ripped a huge hole in the side of the rogue's neck with her mouth and then dove back in for more as the rogue tried his best to roll away from her.

But that deadly tail of hers wasn't finished with him yet. This time it whipped out and caught the rogue's carapace, slicing a huge ugly cut through it like it was so much warm butter.

The rogue thrashed even harder, but he was clearly mortally wounded.

"Kill that bitch!" the Professor shouted, stepping even closer to the fight. "Grace, cut her down!"

Grace stepped up beside the Professor and the Kramer opened up, steady as a rock in Grace's hands. With a full clip she sprayed the queen with deadly shots.

The huge queen roared as she ripped another huge hole in the rogue's neck.

Grace finished the first clip and then at an al-

most invisible speed ejected it and put another in.
But as her attention was focused for a second
down at the gun, the queen took advantage.

As if she were swatting a pesky fly, the queen
whipped her tail around and caught Grace square
in the chest with the razor-sharp point, slicing
through her body armor and lifting her high into
the air, cutting her in half and then smashing her
against the stone wall like an egg dropped on a
sidewalk.

White fluid splattered everywhere, dripping
down the alien saliva columns and pooling around
her on the floor.

She ended up in three parts.

Her chest and right arm landed on a crushed
alien egg.

Her head, still attached to one shoulder and
arm, bounced off a wall and landed near the Professor.

Her lower torso ended two meters away from
her head, her legs spread like a ten-dollar prosti-
tute's, armor ripped away showing her perfect pubic hair for the alien world to see. Her knees, in
automatic reaction, went up and down, up and
down, like she was asking everyone to look.

On the stump of her neck, where the rest of her
body used to be, white tubes pumped her last
fluid out onto the floor of the queen's chamber.

Quickly the Professor stepped over to her head.
"Grace," he shouted. "God damn it. How'd you let
this happen?"

She opened her eyes and looked at him. "You're
a real ass," she said, "but I suppose you already
knew that."

"Grace?" the Professor said, but she closed her eyes and inside her neck the last of the fluid ran out onto the stone floor.

Behind him the queen screamed, then sunk her teeth again into the rogue.

22

Joyce couldn't believe what she was seeing when Kent tossed those two double doors open. She had expected to see a wide-open area with the deck and her shuttle sitting there. Instead what she saw looked like an anthill of bugs, damn near blocking any vision of the shuttle at all. The smell of rot had swept in over them.

In the first few seconds of the fight she and the rest had taken out a good two dozen of the closest and now had cleared every bug out to fifty meters. She'd used six full clips and the Kramer was starting to heat up in her hands.

Kent and his three men had gone out and left, checking the wall above them first. Then Hank and his three had gone out and gone right along the wall, doing the same. That spread out their firing angles and gave them a larger killing area.

She was kneeling beside the door on the right, carefully taking aim and killing any bug that even pretended to move. The rest of the group had spread around the door and were doing the same. It was now starting to feel to her like a target practice session as they all knocked legs and heads off of anything out in that open hangar.

She desperately wanted to get across that killing field of alien bodies and acid blood, but for the moment it felt much safer right where they were, their backs to the wall killing anything that moved in front of them.

Then, through the almost deafening bursts of gunfire around her, she heard her name being shouted. "Captain Palmer! Captain Palmer!"

She stood and looked both directions down the line. Hank and a few others had heard the call also and had stopped firing. He indicated the voice had come from the right, closer to the main entrance and above him. She stepped out and looked up at the balcony that ran along there. It was dark and she couldn't see a thing.

"Cease fire!" she shouted. "Cease fire, unless one moves right at you!"

The firing stopped and the last of the roaring sound echoed over the dead aliens and the hangar deck.

"Captain Palmer?"

"Right here," she shouted back.

"Sergeant Green up here."

"Glad to hear your voice, Sergeant," Joyce shouted back. The relief of having the Marines with them again was almost as much as she had felt when they first showed up in the tunnels.

"You need to get to your ship as soon as you can," Green called back.

To her left a Kramer opened up and across the deck an alien head exploded like a cherry bomb going off. She waited until the echo died off in the huge chamber, then shouted back, "We were headed that way."

"I know," Green said. "But a pitched fight like this will only draw more bugs to this area. There's more of them than you have bullets to kill. Trust me."

"What should we do?" Joyce shouted, feeling relieved she had someone else to make the decisions for a moment.

"Fan out in small groups," Green shouted, "then fight your way to the ship. We'll cover you from here."

"Will do," she said.

"Back to plan A," she shouted at Kent and Deegan to her left. "Let's move. Hank, you ready?"

"Right, with you," he said.

She motioned for the men around her to follow her, pointing to three of the men near her. "You watch our asses. Don't let one of those sons of bitches in behind us. Understood?"

All three nodded.

She clicked a fresh clip into her Kramer and took a deep breath. Then started off slowly toward her shuttle, across the field of dead bugs and acid blood.

All around her Kramers screamed and bugs died.

From the balcony behind her Kramers cut the

air, blowing aliens away at incredible distances across the huge hangar. Those Marines were great shots, of that there was little doubt.

She caught a glimpse of one of the downed aliens in front of her twitching and she blew its head apart like a melon hitting a wall.

Another bug crawled up on her ship over the hatch they were headed for and she and two others beside her sent it spinning off the other side in an acid spray. Joyce hoped like hell that acid didn't get into any important mechanisms on the outside of the shuttle. She didn't think it would, but anything was possible.

On her left the sounds of firing were continuous. She glanced over and Deegan's group was in position approaching the nose of the shuttle. They were firing more often than any, keeping the bugs away from the ship and watching their open left side.

Twenty meters closer to her, Kent and his group paralleled her, mostly helping Deegan's group keep the left clear.

Twenty meters to her right Hank and his crew, supported by help from Sergeant Green above and behind them, had very little to do.

She made the ramp and stationed two men at the bottom and two others to watch the top of the ship above her. She scrambled up the ramp and was damn glad to see the door had been sealed. She let out a deep sigh and started the opening cycle. At least inside would be bug free.

She got the door open and then turned back to check on everybody's position.

Deegan and his men were posted around the

nose of the shuttle, watching both sides of the ship.

Hank and his men were doing exactly the same around the tail and thruster section. The rest had taken up positions around the ship, killing any bug that moved anywhere, sometimes two or three men taking it out with long-distance shooting.

"Sergeant!" Joyce shouted. "Join us. We'll cover you."

"On our way," Green's voice echoed over the chamber.

"Hurry, God damn it," she said under her breath. "Hurry."

She had a sinking feeling that everything was about to go very wrong. She didn't know why. Everyone was in place and no bug was getting within fifty meters of the ship. But it still felt wrong, like it had been too easy.

And Green's words echoed in her head about her not having more ammunition than bugs. She still had two belts left.

The five Marines were down the stairs from the balcony and spread out in an arrow formation, with Green in the center, jogging across the floor through the dead bugs when things changed.

And changed quick.

"Bugs through the storage area!" Kent shouted as the door to the labs smashed inward with a huge crash and a wave of black, ugly aliens swarmed through the brightly lit storage room.

Kent, and some of the men around him who had the best shots straight into the room, opened fire, cutting some of the bugs down under the bright lights before they could even get to the hangar doors.

But there were so many more bugs behind them. They just kept coming, climbing right over the bodies of their dead like they weren't even there.

"Green! Behind you!" Hank shouted.

The entrance to the decontamination chamber was suddenly filled with bugs swarming through like a dam had just broken.

Green and his men, still only halfway to the ship, spread out and took up positions, their guns screaming, filling the entrance and the decontamination chamber with dead aliens.

But the flow of bugs continued, through both doors and from the overhead balcony where the sergeant and his men had just been a few moments before.

And from the shadows of the far side of the hangar.

Clip after clip, she cut down bugs, reloaded, cut down more.

Reloaded.

Cut down more.

And they just kept coming.

And coming.

The Kramer felt like a hot pan in her hands, but she held on. She didn't have time to let it cool. Her ears were ringing. The gray smoke from the guns half blinded her.

"Grenades!" Green shouted and almost as one five headed for the main entrance. To her right she saw Kent and three of his men do the same at the entrance from the supply area.

The concussion from the grenades sent alien

limbs, heads, and bodies everywhere and shook rocks from the roof of the hangar deck.

But the bugs just kept coming.

Climbing over hundreds of their own dead, they poured into the room.

"Fall back," Green shouted to his men and they started moving backward, firing as they went.

"Give them cover!" Joyce shouted and she and her crew did the best they could to keep the bugs back.

But it was clear Green and his men weren't going to make it.

Green had been right. There was just too many of them.

But she kept firing anyway.

The queen bit almost completely through the neck of the rogue and the Professor's pride, his creation, his lifetime of work, lay on the floor twitching like so much raw meat.

The queen bent over her victim, grabbed the rogue's remaining arm, and yanked it off, throwing it against the wall as if disgusted.

The Professor was livid. Behind him the remains of Grace were splattered along the wall. He bent and picked up her Kramer, then cocked the Sound Cannon.

"You're dead, you bitch!"

With the Kramer in his left hand, he punched the on button for the Sound Cannon and set it to high. So high it could kill any alien within two hundred meters by itself.

So high she wouldn't know what hit her.

The room seemed to shimmer and the alien

queen reared up, seeming to scream, her hands at her head.

"Don't like that, do you, bitch?" he shouted, firing at her with the Kramer in his left hand, stepping closer and closer.

Her tail smashed the remains of the rogue behind her and she turned away from the sting of the bullets, still screaming her silent scream.

He pumped bullets at her and stepped closer.

As she swung around, away from his painful attack, her razor-sharp tail went up and then down at the Professor.

Her aim was perfect, and lightning fast.

He saw it coming, but didn't have time to move even a fraction of a meter.

The impact knocked him sideways and sent him spinning across the floor to the left. The pain in his side and arm didn't seem real, it was so sharp. He could feel his blood pumping into the air.

His right arm, cut off cleanly at the shoulder with the Sound Cannon still gripped tightly in his right hand, flew through the air and landed near Grace.

It bounced once, but the impact served to jar the finger even more into the trigger.

The Professor screamed and tried to stop the blood flowing from the hole in his shoulder.

The queen screamed and tumbled sideways, her legs and tail smashing what was left of the rogue.

Beside Grace the Sound Cannon with the Professor's arm still attached started beeping.

Slow at first, but then faster and faster.

Through gritted teeth the Professor laughed.

"It's going critical, you bitch. You're going to die for what you did."

Beep! Beep! Beep!

The queen continued thrashing.

Beep-beep-beep-beep.

"Oh, does that hurt, my dear?" the Professor cried. He tried to sit up but couldn't. "I sure hope so."

The beeping of the gun turned into a long, continuous high-pitched wail as the Sound Cannon went critical.

"I'll see you in hell, bitch!"

The intense white flash ended his insanity.

And her pain.

23

The sound of over twenty automatic Kramers firing almost continuously filled the hangar deck around Joyce like the roar of a river crashing over a hundred-meter falls. The echoes combined with the actual sound and intensified it, banging at her from all sides. She had sweat running down her hands and the Kramer was so hot she could hardly hold it.

She stood, her back against the door frame to her shuttle, aiming and firing.

Then loading, aiming, and firing again.

And then again and again and again at the mass of black bugs climbing over the bodies of other smashed black bugs.

But no matter how many bugs they killed, the ugly things just kept coming.

Within seconds they were going to overwhelm Sergeant Green and his men.

"Pull back!" she shouted to Hank.

She turned to Kent. "Pull back! Pass the word to Deegan!"

He nodded that he understood as he inserted another clip into his rifle and emptied it into the moving mass of alien flesh.

Then suddenly, as if on a string pulled by one evil puppeteer, every live alien within sight seemed to twist, as in pain.

Then they all froze.

"What the hell!" Green shouted.

For a few more seconds the Kramers cut down the frozen bugs where they stood, then the firing slowed and stopped.

"Looks like a Sound Cannon got them, Sarge!" one of the Marines near Green shouted. Joyce couldn't tell which one it was and she had no idea what a Sound Cannon was, but if it could stop these bugs, it was a good thing.

"But we don't have a damn Sound Cannon."

"Well, someone does," Green shouted. "And they may or may not know how to use it. Everyone in the shuttle. Fast!"

Joyce was amazed at how fast some of those tired people could move. She was inside first, her Kramer beside her pilot seat, already starting everything up when Deegan drove into the copilot's seat beside her.

She glanced around at where Hank was crouched, watching the scene outside the door as the five Marines poured inside.

Green stepped through the door, a look of panic on his face. "McPhillips! Dillon! Young! Check the ship for any bugs. Double quick."

Then he turned to Joyce.

"They moving out there yet?" she asked.

"Not yet," Green said, "and if they don't soon, whatever Sound Cannon that's doing this is going to go critical and blow every seal in this base right into space. Those things never work for longer than a minute. How fast can you get us out of this dump?"

"Do it, Deegan!" She didn't even wait to give Green an answer. The total look of panic on his face was more than enough to let her know they didn't have enough time as far as he was concerned.

"Seal the hatch!" she shouted, but both Hank and the sergeant were already working to do just that.

"Engines coming up!" Deegan shouted. "Everything green. Bay door opening. Counting it down."

"Screw the countdown!" she shouted. "Just pray I miss the damn doors on the way out."

Her fingers flew over the board in front of her as the rumble under her seat increased.

Part of that was the ship and the normal vibrations from liftoff. She knew that feeling better than anything. But there was something more happening.

Something much more. It was as if the entire base was shaking.

In one quick motion she swung the nose of the shuttle off the ground and around toward the slowly opening bay doors. There might be enough room to get through if she hit it perfectly. What the hell choice did she have?

The shaking grew more intense around her and between the shuttle and the hangar doors rocks started to fall from the ceiling.

"Everyone hang on!" she yelled.

She hit the acceleration hard.

It shoved her back into her seat and held her there like a hand on her chest. Behind her she could hear a few oaths from those not braced tightly enough. Rocks pounded against the shuttle as the roof of the hangar started to cave in, but she paid no attention. Only those half-open hangar doors were what mattered now.

With the huge shuttle she took aim.

And hoped.

She missed the doors on both sides by meters as the shuttle cleared the hangar and broke into space. With a hard yank she sent the shuttle up in as steep an ascent as she thought the thrusters could handle. She wanted to put some distance between them and that rock.

Deegan swore beside her as his fingers danced over the board in front of him as he did his best to help where she needed him.

"Rearview monitors," she shouted through the incredible noise of the acceleration.

Somehow Deegan managed to get the screen above them focused on the hangar doors. She would never forget what those doors looked like exploding outward into space.

Another few seconds and they wouldn't have made it.

That was close. Too damn close.

She eased the acceleration back slightly and

turned to Deegan. "Think you can get us into a low parking orbit without my help."

Deegan, his face white, the Kramer still draped across his lap, looked at her. His eyes were wide and sweat was pouring off his forehead.

He swallowed, glanced around at the board in front of him, and then back at her. Then he let out a deep breath like he had been holding it for the last ten minutes. "Yeah, I can get us there."

"No walk in the park?" she asked, half smiling.

He glanced at her. "Boss, I've decided working with you is never a walk in the park."

She laughed, also exhaling for what seemed like the first time in hours.

She turned to where Hank and Sergeant Green were braced against the acceleration on the bulk-head behind her.

"Now," she said, "would someone please tell me what the hell just happened?"

"We got out alive," Green said.

Hank glanced at Joyce and then at the monitor over his head. "Yeah, but about fourteen hundred didn't."

24

"This is Captain Palmer of the transport vessel *Caliban* giving a final, pre-cold-sleep status report."

Joyce flicked off the recording and looked around her now silent ship. Sleep chambers, lined up in two rows, head to head, filled the center core of the vessel. It seemed so peaceful and quiet after the past week, with everyone sleeping.

She ran her hand over Hank's chamber, looking down at the peaceful expression on his face. Very soon they would start a new life together. Very soon she would see Drake and Cass, see how much they had grown, how much they had matured.

She did a slow check of the instruments above

Hank one last time. All seemed to be in order and all lights were green, so she turned back to her board and flicked on the recording mike again.

"We have left orbit over Charon Base and I have set course to rendezvous with Moreno Station in eight months. Everyone is in cold sleep and all lights are green."

She took a slow, deep breath, shivering slightly in the cold from being so close to so many sleep chambers. She was wearing only a T-shirt and brief bikini bottoms. That was why she was cold. Or maybe it was from the thought of going into cold sleep shortly herself.

She glanced at her open sleep chamber and then she went on.

"As I have logged, we maintained orbit over Charon Base looking and hoping for more survivors, but we found none, with nothing but static on all frequencies from the base. Sergeant Green thinks the explosion that broke the base containment and collapsed many of the tunnels, at least from what we could scan, was caused by a Sound Cannon going critical in the heart of the alien section. Check his report for more."

She stopped recording and slowly walked back through the ship to the control area.

She always hesitated going into cold sleep with every trip, but this time it seemed even worse. She just couldn't fully understand that the nightmare was over. Every night since their escape into orbit she had had nightmares of bugs crawling out of an airlock or out of a sleep chamber.

But Green and his men had thoroughly scanned both the insides and the outside of the ship and no bugs were with them. Green even put all of them, including himself, through a full body scan to make sure none were implanted.

So she had to believe that for now this fight in this small out-of-the-way section of space, this nightmare, was over.

The aliens had won.

She sat for a moment in her captain's chair staring out at the tiny flecks of stars in front of the ship.

She supposed that the failure had been inevitable. Mankind's prized intellect, in this case, had become its greatest conceit. Out here, in the huge emptiness of space, humans dressed themselves in technology and then thought it made them omnipotent.

Out here the aliens' only function was to reproduce and survive.

Humans called them evil, yet placed men like Professor Kleist in power.

What was truly evil? She didn't know. She just knew a lot of people had died.

With one final glance to make sure all lights on the boards were showing green, she ambled back to the sleep chambers and stood over Hank's for a moment.

Fourteen hundred people dead, yet she and Hank had lived. She hoped that meant good things for their future. She was going to do everything in her power to make sure it did.

It was time to get to sleep and dream about the green of the park and the warmth of the bright sunshine and making love to Hank until she was sweating so hard that the sheets were soaked.

Those were good dreams.

And she could dream about their future. It would be a warm dream, too.

When she and Hank got back to Earth the first thing she would do was take the kids to that park again, no matter how big they had grown since she left.

And she would sit in the warm sunshine.

And she would make love to Hank.

"Good dreams," she said, patting his chamber.

Then she reached down and flipped on the report button.

"This is Captain Joyce Palmer of the transport vessel *Caliban* signing off."

ABOUT THE AUTHORS

SANDY SCHOFIELD is the pen name for the award-winning husband and wife writing team of Dean Wesley Smith and Kristine Kathryn Rusch. Under the Schofield name they have written a number of books, including the popular STAR TREK: DEEP SPACE NINE novel called *The Big Game*. Also writing together they just finished the very first original STAR TREK: VOYAGER novel called *The Escape*.

Kristine Kathryn Rusch is a Campbell and Locus award-winning author who has sold fifteen novels. Her solo novels will come out from NAL, Dell, and Bantam over the next few years as well as uncounted numbers of short stories. She is also the editor of *The Magazine of Fantasy and Science Fiction* and has been nominated the past four years for the Hugo for Best Editor. In 1989 she won the World Fantasy Award for her editing and in 1994 she won the Hugo Award for Best Professional Editor in the world.

Dean Wesley Smith has also sold a large number of short stories and eight novels. His first solo novel, while marketed as science fiction, made it to the final ballot of the Stoker Award. He is also the publisher and editor for Pulphouse Publishing and *Pulphouse: A Fiction* magazine. In 1989, along with Kristine Kathryn Rusch, he won the World Fantasy Award for his work on Pulphouse and the Locus Award for his editing. He has also been nominated four times for the Hugo Award for his editing. He has just finished work on a Spider-Man novel for Berkley Books.